Starless

Amanda Shiffer

Contents

Chapter 1

Under the bright, pulsing lights of the nightclub, his gaze scanned the room. He was hunting that night, yearning for someone interesting to take his mind off the irritating details of his current life. So far, after sitting nursing one beer for nearly half an hour, not a single man had caught his eye. Everyone seemed so... plain.

"Not having much luck tonight, are you, mate?" the bartender sympathized, his thick Northern English accent slowly grating on Kyree's nerves.

"Doesn't look like it," Kyree's voice was much silkier, his accent American and his pronunciation creating a softer, smoother tone.

"Well, 'ere, this might get your motor going," the bartender filled a small shot glass with what looked like vodka and slid it in front of Kyree, "on the house," he added when Kyree cocked an eyebrow. With a small shrug, Kyree knocked back the shot, coughing a little as the strong liquid burned the back of his throat.

"Steady on there, big boy, the night is young," a different voice, laced with a seductive tone, drifted into Kyree's ear as a man sat opposite him, grazing his hand over Kyree's knee. Now, this had been what Kyree was searching for.

Although the lighting in that particular establishment was pretty damn atrocious, Kyree could easily see the swirling greyish blue of the man's eyes, filled to the brim with mystery and intrigue. His dark, straight locks were moulded to perfection, styled just enough to look messy yet not out of place.

"And my night just got a whole lot better, can I buy you a drink perchance?" the man gladly accepted Kyree's offer, ordering some sort of hilariously named and complicated to make cocktail. Kyree liked the man's lips, full and luscious, curved in just the right way to portray both a smirk and a soft smile. He would prefer to see them a little lower than eye level though.

"I'm Ambrose," the man held out his hand which Kyree happily grasped. They both had equally strong handshakes, but Kyree concluded that Ambrose had much softer hands, the hands of someone who didn't partake in a lot of manual labour. He couldn't help imagining how his hands would feel against his skin elsewhere, just the thought was getting him a little too excited.

"Kyree. Ambrose, like from the bible? Heavenly food or something along those lines?"

"Yes," Ambrose tilted his head to the side just a fraction, a hint of shock and bemusement flickering across his face, "I wouldn't have thought a man like you would have known much about the bible."

"A man like me?" it was Kyree's turn to convey confusion as he sipped the beer he had barely touched and was no longer interested in.

"Gay, I mean, not a lot of homosexuals are religious. I certainly am not," Kyree chuckled softly, causing those beautiful lips of Ambrose's to curve even further into a warmer smile.

"How do you know I'm gay?"

"You're in a gay bar, for one, and..." Ambrose leant in close, brushing his fingertips over Kyree's thigh and lowering his volume to a whisper, "you got pretty damn hard the second I walked over," Kyree clicked his tongue quietly, a wicked smirk forming on his own lips.

"You got me there, but since you admit my state of arousal is all down to you, it would only be fair if you took care of it," Kyree suggested, taking his turn to stroke his fingertips down the velvet skin of Ambrose's arm. Ambrose swayed his head left to right a few times as if lost in thought and contemplating Kyree's offer, even though Kyree could clearly see the smirk he was attempting to suppress.

"Tempting, but I just met you, isn't that a little bit dangerous?" Kyree chuckled, a little more sinister this time.

"Who doesn't love a bit of danger?" Kyree rose to his feet, throwing down a couple of notes to pay for the drinks, not really caring about change, just aching to be alone with Ambrose, "you coming then? Be a devil, take the risk, I promise I'm not a murderer."

"You live close?" Ambrose asked as they walked down the street together.

"I have an apartment a few blocks away," Kyree replied, clasping Ambrose's hand as they jogged across the road to avoid oncoming traffic.

Back at Kyree's apartment, Ambrose accepted the glass of wine he was offered and was left alone in the living room area as Kyree ventured into the kitchen. Kyree collected two glasses from the top cupboard and a bottle of red wine from the pantry, listening out for Ambrose's movements. His apartment was actually very quiet, however, he could just about hear the faint music coming from his stereo that Ambrose must have turned on.

Suddenly a pair of hands snaked their way around Kyree's waist, immediately landing on his belt. He could feel Ambrose's hot breath on his neck as he focused on trying not to fumble too much with the leather belt.

"Eager, aren't we?" Kyree breathed, spinning around in Ambrose's grasp so he was chest to chest with him. Their lips crashed together, with Ambrose's tongue instantly invading Kyree's mouth, his hands never pausing in their efforts to remove his jeans.

Kyree grasped a fistful of Ambrose's dark locks, satisfied when he heard a soft moan rumble from his throat and felt his hands finally remove the belt. His other hand trailed under the dark shirt covering Ambrose's muscled form, kneading the firm flesh of his hips and sides.

Ambrose pulled back slowly, a smirk once again on his red raw lips as he dropped to his knees in front of Kyree. Kyree mirrored that same smirk as Ambrose dove his hand into his exposed black boxers, his touch sending a surge of pleasure throughout his body.

Kyree wanted to tell him how amazing it felt, what his touch did to him, but all that left his lips was a succession of straggled groans as Ambrose replaced his hand with his mouth. Once again, collecting a fistful of Ambrose's hair, and hearing that strained moan, Kyree began moving in sync with Ambrose.

Just as he reached the edge of his climax, Ambrose cut all physical contact with him, leaving him there, on the precipice. An almost growl left Kyree's lips, mixed in with a whine, as Ambrose rose to his feet, licking his lips.

"Mmm don't want it to all be over yet, do we? We've not even got to the good part," Ambrose clasped Kyree's hand, spun on his heels, and led him to the bedroom as if it were his apartment, not Kyree's.

The second they entered Kyree's bedroom, Ambrose had him pinned to the wall, his mouth buried in his neck. Kyree moaned and groaned, tugging off Ambrose's shirt and running his fingers down the smooth yet rock hard muscles covering his chest. Neither could wait any longer, both too eager to drown themselves in pleasure.

As more clothes ended up tossed around the room, the two moved to the large, oak bed. Ambrose pushed Kyree down onto the mattress, dominating him just as Kyree loved. Ass up, face down, subject to whatever Ambrose desired.

The pleasure was intense, flowing through the men in waves as their bodies moved simultaneously, fitting into one another perfectly. They were loud, it was rough, neither cared.

Ambrose leant down, pressing a line of hurried kisses down Kyree's back, pushing him over the edge finally. Ambrose joined him, all the tension in their bodies unwinding together. Breathless, they simply collapsed on the bed, tangled in a mess of limbs and sheets, falling into a slumber so quickly neither even had the chance to notice the darkness that had taken over both sets of their eyes.

Morning rolled around too fast, Kyree thought as he was roused from his sleep by the bright light streaming through the partially open curtains. His body was aching, that warm pain that clung to him after a night like last night, he loved it. He caught sight of Ambrose in just his dark jeans, scanning the room in search of his shirt obviously.

"Leaving so soon?" Kyree asked, sitting up and tugging the bunched up covers further over his bare legs that were beginning to feel the chill of the cool room.

"Oh, you're awake," Ambrose smiled but Kyree had seen the soft grimace on his face, "I was hoping to leave whilst you were still asleep, I've never been good with the morning after these nights," who was?

"Have breakfast with me first, I would hate to think of you paying for some overpriced meal when I could easily make you one. Unless, you have somewhere to be," glancing at his expensive-looking gold watch, Ambrose shook his head.

"I have a meeting at eleven so really I need to be on my way at half ten. I can stay for breakfast if you really want," Kyree rose to his feet from the bed, allowing the covers to fall away from his naked body, stretching his arms above his head. He didn't care about Ambrose seeing his manhood, after all, that had been the intention of the night before.

"I insist," Kyree stepped over to the wardrobe, pulling on a pair of dark grey sweatpants and a white t-shirt. Out of the corner of his eye, he could see Ambrose staring at him, that same lustful expression on his face from the previous night. The t-shirt Kyree had decided upon for the day hugged his body, flaunting his defined muscles under the thin fabric.

Kyree merely chuckled as Ambrose followed him into the kitchen, knowing full well his pretty grey-blue eyes were glued to his ass. It was only 10, so Kyree knew he had another half an hour with Ambrose before he had to leave. Just enough time to make breakfast and act interested.

"So, you work?" Kyree knew the difficulties of making small talk the morning after a night like the one Ambrose and he had shared but attempted some anyway. Cracking an egg into a frying pan, he watched as it sizzled, the hot oil spitting at him, yet not burning him at all as it clung to his skin. The droplets were so small Kyree knew Ambrose wouldn't have noticed, still, he angled his body to block his bare arms from Ambrose's view. Just in case.

"Yeah, I'm high up in some political business," well that was surprisingly vague, Kyree wondered if he would ever need to use the acts of the previous night as some form of blackmail. He wasn't like that, but his mind had wandered absently to the idea.

"Politics? Sounds very..." Kyree wanted to say intriguing, his mouth even began to form the words, but he didn't like to lie and changed his mind last minute, "tedious," understanding his humour, Ambrose chuckled.

"It has its perks, can be very interesting at times. What about you? You surely can't afford an apartment like this on a low salary job," Kyree placed an omelette in front of Ambrose on the breakfast bar and watched him take his first bite, "this is amazing, thank you. Don't tell me you're a chef?"

"No, I'm..." his job, or future job that he was training for, was difficult to explain so he took a leaf from Ambrose's book, "in the protection business, bodyguards, personal security, something along those lines," inexplicit subtext seemed to be the correct way to broach their equally personal jobs.

The two continued speaking for a further 20 minutes until Ambrose finally had to leave. Usually, Kyree couldn't stand speaking to his lovers the morning after, coaxing them to leave as soon as possible, if they weren't already gone by the time he woke up, that is. Yet, Ambrose was still so intriguing to him, and talking with him was enjoyable, Kyree almost didn't want to let him go.

Kyree pondered asking him to stay another night, wanting to learn more about this man who was so unlike any others. No, that would be foolish. He had to get home, for one, and, for another, his father would not approve of him growing close to someone like Ambrose.

"You've got my number, I hope to see a call from you," Ambrose called back as he left, picking up his jacket on the way out and closing the door gently behind him with a confident smile. Kyree didn't have his number. They both knew that. There would be no call, there would be no bumping into each other in the streets, they would never see one another again. This town was yet another Kyree had to cross off his list for fear of encountering a one night stand.

Locking the door, Kyree stuffed his phone, wallet and keys into his sweatpants pocket, before tugging his leather jacket over his broad shoulders. He didn't care about any of the other clothes he had left there, didn't care about the whole month of rent and the security deposit he had paid. He would not be returning.

And with that thought, Kyree dissipated into nothing, off to his next destination, materialising as any another demon would.

Chapter 2

"You're late," Kyree narrowly avoided the dagger thrown at his head as he appeared in the home gym his father had installed years ago. Shooting a glare at his younger brother, Kyree shrugged off his jacket, removing all items from his pockets so they didn't get broken during his training.

"Don't pout, brother, I was busy. I'm only half an hour late, anyway," Kyree removed the dagger from where it was impaled in the dark stone wall behind him, not wanting to risk his mother entering and see it.

"Who were you screwing this time? Some maths teacher? Or maybe a talent scout? I've lost count of your escapades into the human world," Kyree chuckled at his brother's comment, pulling off his t-shirt to expose his rippling muscles.

"Idella, who I fuck isn't really any of your business. But if you must know, it was a politician in Newcastle. England is terrible this time of year, I don't recommend it," Idella grimaced, causing Kyree to laugh once again as he stepped onto the deep blue mat, standing opposite to his brother, who was tiny in comparison to him.

"Have you ever been with a man for more than one night recently? You might benefit from it, Ky," Idella threw the first punch, aiming for Kyree's jaw, predictable and easy to dodge.

"I'm not a monogamous personality, Idella, you know that," Kyree moved swiftly, landing a low blow to Idella's abs, knocking him off balance for just a second. He easily recovered, sinking a hit to Kyree's side then attempting to hook his leg around his brother's to pull him down.

With Idella's movements faltering slightly, Kyree could easily overpower him, pulling him into a chokehold. Idella struggled for a second, before yielding and tapping Kyree's arm in a signal of defeat.

"There's never been one single guy you've wanted to stay with for more than one night?" Kyree hesitated with his response, debating the thought as he and his brother continued to spar. Ambrose came to mind, the pure enigma he carried with him did fascinate Kyree.

"No," Kyree finally admitted as he sat on his brother's chest, holding down his arms with ease, "I much prefer to have a different suitor every night," Idella squirmed under Kyree, then gave up for the fourth time in a row. Realistically, sparring with his brother was pointless, Kyree was both stronger and smarter than Idella, he always won. Yet he had to keep training, even if there was no real challenge to it.

"Surely you want more, a relationship? A mutual appreciation? Someone to hold at night and wake up to every morning? Someone to love?" although Idella didn't realise, Kyree had thought about that a lot. He pondered love often, yearning for it every night he ventured to the human world, but instead filling the empty hole with meaningless sex.

"You don't have that, you seem fine," Kyree wasn't mocking his brother's lack of love, just as Idella wasn't mocking Kyree's lifestyle. He was merely making a point as his brother tapped out once again.

"I don't sneak into the human world every other night to satisfy that need, you're the one that deals with your problems incorrectly."

"Idella, I don't sneak into the human world. I'm 685 years old, it's not sneaking when you're over 6 centuries old, I'm not a teenager anymore. It's simply-" Kyree was interrupted by the radiant being that was his mother, in a not so radiant mood.

"Kyree Landon! You've been trespassing the human world and fornicating with the males?!" his mother scolded, stalking into the room from her position hidden in the doorway. Kyree was sure by the smug look on his brother's face that he had planned the encounter.

"Well when you put it that way, mother, it sounds much worse than the reality," Kyree attempted to bring some sort of humour into the situation but his mother was having none of it. The human world was not permitted for demons, not for recreational purposes anyway, it would have been a serious offence had Kyree's parents not had such important positions in the underworld.

"What do you call it then, Kyree?! How long has this been going on?" just because his mother lowered her voice from a shriek to a more composed volume did not mean her anger had simmered in any way. Kyree opened his mouth to reply, but his brother spoke before him.

"He's been going up there since-" Kyree slapped Idella across the face, silencing him.

"Say his name and we will fight for real on this mat, Idella, I warned you," Kyree seethed, not caring about the red handprint seeping onto his little brother's cheek.

"Oh, Ky," their mother stretched up to cup Kyree's cheek, knowing that the physicality between her sons would be forgotten in minutes, her eyes filled with sorrow, "this isn't how you should be grieving, my sweet, it's been

4 years. I know your heart still hurts but you can't go on living like this, you must move on," Kyree clenched his fists, taking a few breaths to calm himself, not wanting to hurt his mother because of his explosive anger. After a few seconds, he rested his hand atop his mother's, his hazel eyes revealing he was still in so much pain even after nearly 5 years.

"I'm trying, mother, I promise. It helps, honestly," his mother sighed, a mixture of disappointment and regret plastered across her face.

"Ky, it's not healthy. Please, promise you won't go up there anymore. If you got caught or hurt, I..." tears sprung to his mother's eyes and Kyree knew she was imagining his early demise.

"Mother, I'm very careful. I don't show my true self, not to anyone, and I don't frequent the same areas in the same century. Plus, Idella always knows when I'm out, if I didn't return in the morning he would find me."

"Kyree, please, please, promise me you won't go back up there. I know you think it helps but I know for a fact it doesn't. You need to face this issue head-on, not hide away with human men," Kyree's heart ached as his mother pleaded for his safety, but he knew the promise she wanted was not one he could keep. Nevertheless, if it put her mind at ease...

"OK, mother, I promise. I won't go back up there," until tomorrow night, Kyree continued in his head, knowing he would be driven insane without the empty pleasure of human men.

"Anyway," his mother removed her hand from his cheek, changing the subject to something more important, "I came down to remind you both that we will be having a guest staying with us for the unforeseeable future. Your father wants you both at dinner tonight on your best behaviour to meet him."

"Do we not get to know who this man is until tonight?" Kyree queried, not as content as his brother with secrecy.

"My sweet, not even I know who this man is. Only your father knows. He told me it is very important and that this man must feel welcomed into our home for the duration of his stay," his mother smiled, kissing her son's hands in turn, no longer tall enough to reach their cheeks without them bending down, "I will let you return to your training now. Dinner is at 5, do not be late," with that, Kyree's mother spun on her heels and exited the room through the door she had entered.

"A guest, a male guest, how interesting..." Kyree muttered to himself, a small smirk tugging at the corners of his mouth.

"You're not thinking of fucking him, are you, Ky?" Idella responded with an exasperated tone, making Kyree chuckle deeply.

"Well, mother doesn't want me in the human world, and she wants him welcomed. Sounds like a win-win situation to me."

Kyree stepped into the shower at 4:00, marvelling in the feeling of the hot water hitting his aching flesh. He craved the peace of a shower after a night in the human world, washing away any remnants of the man he had been with. His scent, his touch, anything. As much as he enjoyed their company, he didn't need the memories to remain for long.

For a while, Kyree stood in the shower, listening to the sound of the water droplets pummeling against his tanned skin. His thoughts had drifted to who the mystery man that was staying with them was. He did not like secrets, and he did not like anticipation. Kyree liked to know everything up front, that way there would be nothing to come back to bite him in the ass. Not that he didn't like being bitten in the ass.

When Kyree finally exited his shower at 4:30, he felt considerably more relaxed. His shoulders no longer tense and the ache in his muscles only a dull pain, much more bearable. Maybe eating dinner with his family for once would not be such a tedious and irritating task.

Kyree had many suits in his wardrobe, all expensive and tailored especially for him. For that night, he had chosen deep blue slacks, with a blazer of matching colour and a stark white shirt underneath. He finished the outfit with a powder blue tie, styling his hair and glancing in the mirror just as his mother shouted for him to come down to dinner.

Kyree exited his room the same time as his brother, who was wearing a light grey suit with a deep maroon tie. Thankfully, the suit covered his sleeves of tattoos, so there would be no tutting from their mother that night. Hopefully.

"Looking good, little brother," Kyree nodded curtly toward his brother as they made their way down the marble stairs.

"As do you, big brother," Idella replied as they entered the kitchen, seeing their mother fretting with the chef.

"Mother, it's best you remain in the living room with father, don't you think?" Kyree coaxed his mother into the room where his father was waiting, hoping she hadn't been too rude to the staff. She was merely flustered, they would get a pay rise for the night for the trouble.

"Oh, my boys," Yennifer gushed as she finally caught sight of her two sons next to her husband, "you all look so handsome," Yennifer was wearing a beautiful mauve gown that just skimmed the floor at her feet. It hugged her perfect figure, with the back stopping midway down her spine, exposing more of her smooth, tanned skin.

Kyree's father, Orion, was dressed in a dark grey suit, with a mauve tie matching his wife's dress. Kyree knew his mother had dressed him, his father had no sense of fashion, despite constantly spouting that they must always look their best at all times.

"Sir," a timid voice chimed in from the doorway, grasping the attention of the small demon family. One of the new maids, whose name Kyree had already forgotten, hovered in the doorway awaiting permission to continue.

"Yes, Melissa?" Kyree didn't know how his father managed to remember every name of all the staff in the mansion, it was impossible to him.

"Your guest is here, Sir, he's waiting in the foyer with two other men," Orion thanked Melissa and waved her away.

"Let us go welcome our guest. Kyree, Idella, behave," Orion warned as he took his wife's hand and led his sons to the foyer. Three men were stood awaiting the Landon family's arrival. The two on either side of the third were facing the direction the Landon's had entered, wearing white suits with black ties.

The third, the man in the middle, was facing away from the family, examining the foyer. The suit he wore was jet black, and fit him very nicely, thought Kyree as his eyes wandered over the man. His brows furrowed suddenly as a ripple of recognition hit him, he knew that ass.

"Yennifer, Kyree, Idella," Orion began as the man turned and Kyree's eyes widened at the sight of him, "meet Ambrose Ross, next in line to the throne."

Chapter 3

The shock stimulated a sort of hysteric reaction in Kyree. He tried his hardest to suppress the laugh bubbling up within him, covering his mouth, even acting as though it was a cough. Nothing worked, his nerves transferring the anxiety to hilarity within him.

Ambrose didn't seem to be having the same reaction. His lips, God they brought back memories, were pursed in a straight line, his jaw clenched as he stared right past Orion to Kyree.

"Your majesty, this is my wife Yennifer, my youngest son Idella and my eldest Kyree," his father trailed off when he noticed Kyree struggling to contain himself, "something funny, Kyree?" he glowered at his son for acting so immature in front of their guest.

"I apologise profoundly," Kyree forced out between laughs, trying to compose himself, "it's nothing, I promise," Idella shared in the number of people glaring at Kyree, finally deciding his brother had gone mad.

"Excuse my brother and I," he flashed Ambrose a nervous smile and gripped Kyree's arm, dragging me back to the kitchen, "what the fuck is wrong with you?" he hissed as Kyree continued to giggle like a five-year-old.

"You don't understand-"

"No, you don't understand, Ky. You're acting like an idiot in front of the next king of hell, the man you're training to protect. How do you think this makes you look? How do you think this makes father look? Why are you-"

"Idella, that's the 'politician' I was with last night!" Kyree burst out, still chuckling despite his brother's overtly surprised expression.

"You fucked the prince of hell?" Kyree shrugged, a smirk on his lips.

"Well, he fucked me actually," Idella simply gawped at him.

"What is wrong with you? Do you realise what you've done? You have sabotaged everything you've been training toward, if anyone found out the personal connection you have-"

"Woah," Kyree held up a hand, silencing his babbling baby brother, "we don't have a 'personal connection', Idella. We screwed, a few times, one night together, that's all. I'm not suddenly in love with him or anything," Kyree had to admit he did contemplate the night with Ambrose a little more frequently earlier that day than most others. Yet, he was not in love with him, he knew that for sure.

"Screwing him is a personal connection, Ky, this could really come back to bite you in the ass," using humour as a substitute for any and all other emotions, Kyree allowed the smirk to rise back up onto his face.

"He can bite me in the ass any day, you know I-" Kyree stopped abruptly as his mother entered the kitchen, fury in her eyes, "now, mother, I can explain-"

"Kyree Landon, what is wrong with you lately? First, visiting the human world, now disgracing yourself in front of His majesty. Are you insane?"

"Mother, I will go apologise to him now and be on my best behaviour. OK? Just ask father to help you in the kitchen for 5 minutes and I will make it up to you all," Kyree's smirk had faded to a soft smile, the one he knew broke down his mother's anger every time.

"5 minutes, young man," she concurred, entering back into the living room where Orion was stood speaking to Ambrose. Kyree followed, suppressing the smirk that threatened to take over his face once again. Whispering something in her husband's ear, Yennifer managed to remove him from the room, leaving Kyree alone with Ambrose and the two other men.

"Politician, huh?" Kyree was the first to speak, but Ambrose didn't seem to be finding the situation amusing at all.

"I thought you were human," Ambrose seethed, his eyes that soulless black that Kyree found oh so very attractive in demon men, "if I had known what you were, last night would not have happened."

"And you think I knew about you? How could I? Your father keeps you locked up in that castle all your life, barely anyone knows your face. I didn't intend to bed a demon last night, hence going up to the human world," Kyree retorted, only seeming to anger Ambrose more with the smirk he allowed to slip onto his face.

"Are you seriously finding this funny? Kyree, this kind of thing could ruin me, ruin your family too if it got out," Kyree had no idea why Ambrose was acting so serious about the situation, he found it utterly laughable.

"Why's that? It's not like demon couples aren't allowed, and homophobia down here is at a minimum. What are you so afraid of?" Ambrose sighed, glancing down at the silver ring on his finger.

"I'm to be married, Kyree, when I'm coronated. This marriage is very important to my father and my family. If people found out I snuck into the human world to have a one night stand months into my engagement,

I could be rejected from royalty. My sister would take the throne instead. Your father could lose his status too if anyone found out it was you I was with," it was Kyree's turn to feel the burn of rage.

"You're engaged? You cheated on someone with me? God, do you have no heart? That's awful-"

"It's beside the point, Kyree," Ambrose broke in before Kyree's voice rose too high, "you cannot tell anyone about last night, I'm serious."

"Do you not want to marry him? Is that why you went to the human world? Are you being forced into this?" Ambrose sighed, pinching the bridge of his nose as he felt a headache rolling in.

"No, Kyree, I love him dearly. I made a mistake. We argued and I wanted to spite him. That's all, OK?"

"I won't tell anyone," Kyree muttered glumly, feeling increasingly worse about the previous night than he had earlier, "why are you here anyway?" changing the subject was the optimal idea, Kyree wanted to erase that night from his mind as Ambrose seemed so intent on doing.

"Someone is trying to kill me before I'm coronated. Your father offered refuge to me until the assassin has been found. Hence, he was the only one to know my presence here was expected," everything clicked into place and it all made sense to Kyree then.

"I'm training to be a knight of hell, that's why my father offered for you to stay here. He clearly wants you to see my abilities so there's a higher chance that you'll pick me for the job. I'm surprised your father didn't see through his little plot. It's not malicious, simply politics to my father," Kyree explained, shaking his head lightly.

"If you can save my life and keep our secret, you will most definitely be my knight," Ambrose muttered, swirling the glass of red wine in his hand before taking a sip. Kyree knew his time was running out when he heard his mother and father's footsteps growing closer.

"As I was saying," he began in a much cheerier manner, plastering a smile on his face, "I must have had one too many glasses of champagne before you got here. Seeing a man as handsome as you must have triggered a nervous reaction in me, I do apologise, your majesty," Kyree beamed, knowing his mother and father had entered the room and were awaiting Ambrose's reaction.

"Please, call me Ambrose, formalities are not needed here," Ambrose followed Kyree's lead with ease, also allowing his pretty mouth to curve into a warm smile, "and as for first impressions, forget it. I prefer a lighter-hearted setting than a bunch of stiffs in suits, don't feel you can't be relaxed in my presence, here I am merely a guest, not a prince."

Over dinner, the Landon family got to learn more about who was targeting Ambrose, however, no one really knew all that much personal information and details about the assassin, other than it was a man.

"Oh, you poor thing, how long have you had to live with this?" lamented Yennifer, clasping her husband's hand, deeply affected by Ambrose's admittance, "God, if this was happening to Idella or Kyree, I wouldn't know what to do."

"The first attack was a few days after my father announced he was stepping down from the throne. There has been at least one a week since then," Ambrose didn't seem fazed by how many attempts on his life there had been, he was very relaxed talking about it.

"Well, you'll be safe here, Kyree is training to be a knight so if all else fails I'm sure he will protect you. Won't you, Ky?"

"Hm?" Kyree blinked a few times, the mention of his name dragging him back to reality from his daydream, "oh, yeah, of course," Kyree had barely been listening to the conversation around him, too busy daydreaming about the last time he had eaten a meal with his family. He was alive then, happy, in love. He shook himself mentally, not wanting to have any sort of breakdown in front of his family and Ambrose.

"Sir," one of the men in white suits that Ambrose had brought with him interrupted, "there is someone in the garden," the man had been staring out the window during the entire dinner, with the other stood in front of the living room door in case anyone wanted to enter uninvited.

"Kyree," Orion motioned to the garden, wanting Ambrose to see his son in action. Kyree stood immediately, removing his jacket and resting it over the back of his chair. Without a word, he left the room and strode out into the darkness of their garden, completely aware of Ambrose stood at the window watching him.

"This is private property," he called into the darkness, noticing the shadowy figure lingering on the edge of the forest that surrounded his father's mansion, "leave, you shouldn't be here," a melodic laugh trickled into the air, one Kyree found oddly familiar.

"What happened to 'you're always welcome here, Tyrell, don't hesitate to visit'?" Kyree cringed, instantly knowing who the figure was.

"You didn't seriously believe that, did you, Tyrell?" Kyree crossed his arms over his chest as the figure stepped closer to him, "you can't be here tonight, my father is meeting with someone important."

"Oh, come on, Ky, I came to see you. I miss us. I miss what we had," Kyree rolled his eyes at Tyrell's whining tone, a scowl on his face.

"What we had was one night together 3 years ago, we were both lonely and grieving. You were the one that agreed to forget about it, grovelling won't work after all this time," Kyree batted away the hand Tyrell extended to touch him with, "are you fucking drunk? Go home, Tyrell," Kyree's patience was running dry at a faster pace than usual.

"Don't tell me you're seriously still hung up on Alexander, it's been-" Kyree's anger exploded out of him as his fist connected with Tyrell's jaw, sending him stumbling backwards.

"Don't say his name!" Kyree roared, shocking even himself at the amount of fury encased inside his subconscious.

"Saying his name isn't gonna change anything, Kyree! It's not going to bring him back! He's dead! He's dead and it's your fault! You may have lost a fiance that night but I lost a brother, don't you dare act like you're the only one entitled to grief!" Tyrell snarled, holding his jaw.

"Get off this property, Tyrell, if I ever see you here again, I'll kill you," Kyree turned, about to head back into the house, knowing Tyrell wouldn't stick around for fear of being hit again.

"Like you did my brother?" Tyrell spat before Kyree was out of earshot. A twinge of pain spiked through the demon's heart, bringing tears to his eyes.

"Like I did your brother."

Chapter 4

K yree didn't return to the dinner table that night. In fact, he didn't leave his room until a few days had passed. He had to walk Endwin, he had left him to his own devices for days and was subsequently surprised he had chewed through the house. The afternoon was warm, as usual in the underworld, no breeze, just sweltering heat that felt almost suffocating. Kyree used to enjoy walks through the woods, back when he used to enjoy life altogether.

"Endwin, leave it!" Kyree shouted as his dog bent down to sniff some dead animal half buried in decaying leaves. As the dark coloured dog bounded off further into the foliage, Kyree stopped, a carving in a tree catching his eye. It was a heart, a very crudely drawn one with 'K+A' in the middle. Kyree yearned to feel something, anything, even anger at that point would be a privilege. Yet he just felt numb. As if the events of the night a few days ago had sapped any remnants of his soul from his body.

"Who is he?" Kyree flinched at the sound of another voice behind him, glancing over his shoulder at the familiar figure.

"You shouldn't be outside, Ambrose, you're much more vulnerable out here," Kyree grumbled, continuing down the path ahead of him to follow his dog, hoping Ambrose would take his advice and leave him the fuck alone.

"I'm with my knight, I'm sure you'll keep me safe," Ambrose linked his arm into the crook of Kyree's, a soft smile on his face. He was wearing faded blue jeans and a dark green hoodie that looked a few months old. Not the same sense of sophistication radiating from him as the night before.

"Where's your goon squad?" Kyree glanced at Ambrose's arm resting in his, then averted his eyes back to the forest floor.

"You mean Osiris and Anubis? I left them with your father, I told you, I'm with a knight, I expect protection," Kyree didn't bother to respond, honestly not having anything to say to Ambrose. He wasn't in the mood for talking, simply wanting to crawl into a dark hole and sleep for an eternity. The night with Ambrose was the first night in a long time he had a decent sleep, without nightmares scratching at his mind that is.

"So, who is he?" Ambrose repeated, the direction of his gaze impaired by the sunglasses adorning his face.

"Who are you talking about?" Kyree sighed when Ambrose stopped their movement, clasping his hands over Kyree's fists.

"Alexander," he said gingerly, igniting that same anger in Kyree at Tyrell had the other night, "the man that so clearly broke you, who is he?"

"Was," Kyree choked out, taking a few deep breaths in an attempt to calm himself.

"What?"

"Who was he, is more accurate. He's dead, has been for years," Kyree's breaths got deeper and faster as the pain of remembering Alexander unearthed the agony within him he had tried so hard to bury. The forest began to spin as Kyree's body swayed softly.

"Kyree? Kyree, sit down, you're gonna pass out," Ambrose became two men, then three as Kyree's legs started to give out from under him, "Kyree, calm down, it's OK. You're safe," as Kyree sat on the floor, Ambrose kept a hold of his hands, rubbing his thumbs over the back of his knuckles. That soothing gesture aided in calming Kyree, as though Ambrose was brushing away the pain.

"His name was Alexander," Kyree whispered minutes into the silence, unable to lift his gaze to catch Ambrose's, "he was my fiance."

"What happened?" Ambrose asked, sat opposite Kyree on the ground, his legs crossed as he waited patiently for Kyree's story. It took several more minutes for Kyree to collect his thoughts, yet Ambrose didn't rush him like so many others did, simply waited in silence.

"We'd been together for decades, known each other for centuries. I had proposed to him about 3 years earlier," Kyree began, "my father had insisted we waited until the humans accepted same-sex couples more openly, it would make it easier when we were up there then. God, it was my fault, if I had just stood up to my father, he wouldn't have-" Ambrose made small shushing sounds as tears rolled down Kyree's cheeks, sitting closer so their knees rubbed together.

"Kyree, it is not your fault, whatever happened was not your fault."

"Yes it was," Kyree sniffled, finally looking Ambrose in the eye with those beautiful hazel iris' of his, "he went up to the human world to pick my favourite flowers to put them in my suit pocket. I thought he'd left me at the altar. I thought it was all too much for him. So I went up there, to our favourite place, and..." Kyree inhaled a shaky breath, more tears spilling out of his eyes, "he was there. Beaten. Broken. Dead. They had hung him.

Lynched him like he was some criminal all because he loved me. A man. If we had gotten married the way we wanted, eloping like he asked, he might still be alive. It was my fault," Kyree sobbed, covering his face with his hands, not wanting Ambrose to see him so vulnerable.

"Kyree," Ambrose pulled on his fingers gently, "Kyree, look at me, please," when Kyree finally removed his hands, his eyes were puffy and red, "Kyree, his death is not your fault. He made the choice to go up to the human world that day. His last act was an act of immense care and love, you didn't make him go up there. You didn't kill him, his blood is on the hands of the humans. Not you. You need to let this go, Kyree, you can't live like this," Kyree shook his head weakly, not believing the words spilling out of Ambrose's mouth, so similar to all the therapists over the years. Alexander had died because of him, that fact would not ever change.

"Kyree, I want to take you somewhere, will you let me do that?" Ambrose gripped Kyree's arms, taking his weak shrug as a yes.

Suddenly, it was much lighter, yet the temperature had dropped considerably. Kyree squinted in the light, glancing around the area he and Ambrose had appeared in. All colour drained from Kyree's face, his blood freezing in his veins as he came to realise where Ambrose had brought him.

"W-why - How did you -" Kyree stuttered, jumping to his feet as his entire body trembled.

"There was a photo album in the drawer of the room I'm staying in, the only picture left of you and Alexander was under this tree. I assumed this was the favourite place you told me about," Kyree's gaze flickered over the old oak creaking in the soft breeze, tears stinging his eyes as they landed on the spot forever burned by the rope that had stolen his lover from him.

"I-I can't be here, you shouldn't have brought me here," Kyree could feel the panic rising within him, flashes of that day pounding inside his head as he backed away from the God-awful tree.

"Ky, you need to move on, Alexander would want you to move on," panic seeped into anger which, in turn, grew into rage. Ambrose didn't know Alexander, he barely knew Kyree, and had seemed to think that bringing him to the place where Alexander had died would cure him of his pain.

"You don't know what he would want!" Kyree seethed, subconsciously stepping closer to Ambrose, "you didn't know him! You don't even know me! Just because you're royalty doesn't give you the right to dig all this shit up in my life!"

"Ky-"

"Don't call me that," Kyree growled, his eyes darkening until all of the hazel had been snuffed out by black.

"Kyree, you need to calm down. Alexander wouldn't want you to be acting this way-" everything was a blur then. Movements, sounds, everything. When Kyree's focus returned, he was sat on Ambrose's chest, his fists covered in blood. Ambrose's blood. Ambrose was still under him, his beaten and bloodied face contorted into an expression of pain.

"Ambrose?" Kyree whispered, his hands trembling furiously, "N-No, Ambrose," Kyree shook Ambrose's shoulders, hoping to rouse him from whatever state he was in, "please, Ambrose, I'm sorry, please wake up," more tears dripped from Kyree's eyes as Ambrose remained still. Deathly still. Kyree would be executed if anyone found out what he had done. But he couldn't just leave Ambrose there, he would be easy pickings for the man targeting him if Kyree hadn't already completed the man's job for him first...

Chapter 5

"Kyree..." a soft voice cooed in the demon's ear, half rousing him from his broken slumber, "Ky, wake up," he knew that voice, yet couldn't quite place it. His head felt heavy, fuzzy like it was stuffed with cotton wool, still aching as much as it had been when he drifted out of consciousness God knows how long ago.

It took a few seconds for his eyes to focus when he opened them, the dim light making it very difficult to see who was leaning over him. It was a man, not much older than him, with a black eye and bust lip. His heart skipped a beat when realisation hit.

"Ambrose, you're alive," Kyree wrapped his arms tightly around Ambrose's waist, inhaling his scent as he thanked every God he had ever heard of. Ambrose chuckled, running one hand through Kyree's matted locks, rubbing Kyree's back with the other. Abruptly, Kyree pulled away, backing up as far from Ambrose as he could without falling off his bed.

"You can't be here, you can't be near me," Kyree's speech was slurred, probably from the risky mixing of alcohol and whatever else he took the night before, "I hurt you, you need to stay away from me," Kyree's gaze flickered over the cuts and bruises on Ambrose's face, knowing he did that to someone who was only trying to help him simply fueled the self-pity consuming him.

"I deserved it," Ambrose said with a shrug, perching on the edge of the bed, "I pushed you too far too early. We barely know each other and I shouldn't have assumed taking you there would help. I'm sorry," Kyree shook his head, his brows furrowed into a frown as he averted his gaze to his bloodied knuckles.

"Don't apologise, I'm clearly a danger to everyone, I can't control myself anymore. I should just kill myself, it would be safer for everyone," Kyree mumbled, rubbing his aching skull.

"Don't you dare say that. Killing yourself would break your family, and me," Kyree's eyes shot up to meet Ambrose's, "yes, I said it, your death would hurt me. There's nothing wrong with you, you just have a lot of emotions you haven't been dealing with very well. I want to help you with that," Kyree stared at Ambrose in disbelief.

"I could have killed you," Kyree admitted, "I thought I had killed you, you owe me nothing. Nothing but an execution," Ambrose scoffed, shaking his head and sliding close to Kyree on the bed, who backed tighter against the wall.

"You need help, Ky, not any more death. Let me help you," Ambrose rested his hand over Kyree's, a compassionate smile on his lips.

"Why?" Kyree uttered so softly he wasn't even sure if Ambrose heard him, "why offer help to me? I'm nothing," Ambrose sighed, absently tracing his fingertips over the back of Kyree's hand.

"Because I like you," Kyree's frown deepened so Ambrose continued, "I've been struggling with my feelings for you since our night together. I've not felt so alive like I did that night with you in a long time. I like you, Kyree Landon," Kyree's mind couldn't quite grasp that concept. Someone liking him? He knew it wouldn't work, he knew the ability to love had been burnt out of him when he lost Alexander. Yet that didn't stop him from wanting a relationship and commitment to one man more than anything else in the world.

"I-I can't, you can't. I'll hurt you. People close to me die," Kyree's voice shook as tears, once again, welled in his eyes.

"Ky, I understand Alexander's death hurt you deeply. But you can't live forever grieving someone who isn't coming back. You have to move on with your life, even if you don't share the feelings I have for you, at least let me help you get better so that someone can make you as happy again as you once were," the grey-blue iris' of Ambrose's eyes captivated so many emotions Kyree couldn't pick one out to focus on. He didn't fully understand his own feelings for Ambrose, he had lost faith in love so long ago he couldn't recall what it felt like to have feelings for someone. Whilst he mulled it over, he had to change the subject.

"What about your fiance?" Kyree asked softly, staring at Ambrose's hand over his.

"I may have embellished on my feelings for him. I don't love him, he has been a close friend of mine for many years, but we're not in love. My father and his thought it would be a good partnership, despite my fiance not being gay. They didn't care. We agreed, out of pure friendship, when we should have stood up to our fathers," the two men remained silent for a short while, Kyree absorbing all Ambrose had confided, Ambrose awaiting Kyree's judgement on the situation.

"I..." Kyree paused, the words in full sentences in his mind but falling apart when they hit his lips, "I don't know how to love," he whispered, each word said slowly and with so much empathy Ambrose's heart felt as though it might rip in two.

"So we don't start with that. We start with something you know how to do. I'm not asking you to marry me, Ky, I just want to help you first. We can figure out whatever is between us when you're better, OK?" Kyree didn't think it was fair for Ambrose to put himself through this, getting over Alexander would be difficult and he knew it. Yet, he knew he did feel something for Ambrose, even it was only respect and admiration for his sensitivity and patience. He wanted to know him, wanted to grow closer. And if that meant he had to go through the long process of overcoming Alexander's passing, so be it.

"OK," Kyree agreed, dragging his hand through his tangled brunette locks.

"Good," Ambrose rose to his feet, "now go take a cold shower," Ambrose chuckled at Kyree's cocked eyebrow, "you smell like a liquor store, I don't think your parents would appreciate seeing you this way," Ambrose's gaze drifted to Kyree's bare chest as they both stood simultaneously, appreciating his defined muscles.

"Will you be joining me?" Kyree offered, making Ambrose smile as his confident personality seemed to return. Sex was something Kyree had used to drown out the sadness, it was the only thing he truly felt he was good at with another man.

"I don't think a cold shower would be very productive if I was in there with you. You need to sober up," Kyree pouted, but understood Ambrose's point and left to go take that shower.

When Kyree returned, only adorning a towel wrapped loosely around his waist, wet hair dripping onto the carpet, he knew what the book was that Ambrose was holding.

"That the photo album you found in the guest room?" Kyree asked, dropping the towel to the ground as he wandered over to his wardrobe. He didn't care about Ambrose saw him naked, he had already fucked him, there wasn't really much else he hadn't seen.

"Yes," Ambrose replied, his eyes roaming the back of Kyree's bare figure as he dressed.

"Bottom drawer, black book, that's where the rest of the pictures are," Kyree murmured, tugging a black t-shirt on. When he turned back, Ambrose was flicking through the little black book he had kept hidden for so many years. Kyree sat next to him, stopping him on a picture of Alexander laid in bed holding out his hand to the camera with a smirk on his face. Kyree had forgotten how beautiful he was, his pale skin dotted with freckles and sandy brown hair a mess atop his head.

"That was our 20 year anniversary, we went skiing in the Alps," Kyree smiled, not feeling all that sad at remembering the happy times with Alexander. Ambrose flicked to a picture of Alexander sat next to a campfire, sticking his tongue out at the camera.

"One of our first dates as a couple, we went camping in the Tongass National Forest in Alaska. We didn't sleep there though, Alex thought he heard a bear so we left because he was too scared," Kyree actually laughed, only for a second, and very soft, but Ambrose heard that laugh and continued to another photograph. Kyree was down on one knee, with Alexander covering his mouth, they looked to be on a beach somewhere.

"Some coast in Italy, the day I proposed," Ambrose detected the sadness growing in Kyree's voice and decided to shut the album, placing it back in the drawer where he had found it.

"How have you been dealing with your grief?" Ambrose queried, turning so he could face Kyree easier.

"I met you when I was 'dealing with my grief'," Kyree smiled weakly, a little embarrassed.

"Well no wonder your feelings are all messed up, you've taught yourself to associate sadness with the need for intimacy," Ambrose's tone wasn't mocking, which surprised Kyree somewhat. He wasn't judging him for his unhealthy obsessions like so many others did.

"I don't know how to else to deal with it. Something reminds me of Alex, then all the grief comes back and I go up to the human world to search for comfort, I don't know what else to do," Kyree had never opened up to anyone about his issues, it felt odd.

"How long have you been doing this?" Kyree bit his lip, looking away before responding.

"Since a couple weeks after his death. I started off doing it every couple of months, it was more difficult then with the high security keeping us out of the human world. Recently I've gotten to doing it almost every night," Kyree couldn't bear to look Ambrose in the eye, ashamed of his actions. He was basically a free male prostitute.

"Kyree, it's understandable, you have an addiction. With every fix, or in your case with every fuck, the euphoria lasts for a little less time. It's gonna be difficult to wean you off of it but it will happen. Until then, I'm your bed buddy," Kyree watched as Ambrose stripped down to his boxers and slid under the covers, "you crave comfort when you're low, sleeping in the same bed as someone will help with that," Ambrose had that same smirk on his lips as the first night Kyree had met him, a smirk he could not say no to. Kyree stood, removing the clothes he had only put on a few minutes ago and got into bed with Ambrose.

Kyree felt a little awkward, he had never just slept with another man in bed, not without fucking first anyway. Not since Alexander was alive. He didn't really know where to lay, how close he should be, anything.

"Come here," Ambrose patted his chest when he noticed Kyree looking a little overwhelmed, "I won't bite," Kyree rested his head on Ambrose's chest, fidgeting for a few seconds before finally settling in a comfortable position. Sleep was imminent, and so wonderful when held in someone's arms.

Chapter 6

Kyree was awakened by the sounds of a hushed conversation. One voice was Ambrose's, whose arms he still laid in happily, the other was his mother's. Choosing to remain motionless as though he was still asleep, Kyree listened to the two talking.

"Don't worry, Mrs Landon, nothing happened between me and Ky last night. He couldn't sleep so I joined him, that's all," Ambrose's voice was groggy, his mother must have woken him just a few minutes before.

"Ambrose, I have no objections to you having relations with my Kyree. He's just... he's fragile. I don't know if you know about his previous partner-"

"Alexander, yes, I know what happened. I've been trying to help Kyree deal with his grief, that's why he's sleeping with me," Yennifer was silent for a second, obviously taking in what Ambrose had said. Kyree was more taken aback by the anger that didn't surface when his ex-fiance's name was mentioned.

"Oh, well, then thank you. My sweet Ky hasn't been the same since Alexander's passing, maybe you staying here will be a blessing to him as well as to you. If you can find who Ky used to be, my husband and I will owe you more than our lives."

"I hope to do that, Mrs Landon, Kyree deserves happiness," with a few more seconds of silence, Kyree heard the door click shut quietly and sat up, a soft chuckle slipping out of his mouth when he glimpsed the startled look on Ambrose's face.

"You act all tough but you're a sensitive soul, Ambrose, I don't know if that side of you is truly fit to be the king of hell. Rational thought has a tendency to dwindle when sentiment and sensitivity get involved," Ambrose smiled a warm smile at Kyree, his grey-blue eyes glinting in the soft light of the room.

"Being nice does not equate to sentiment and sensitivity. I happen to be very cold when I need to be, Kyree," Kyree shared in Ambrose's smile as he rose from the bed, pulling on some black sweatpants, "where are you going?"

"My job, unlike yours, requires training everyday," Ambrose sat up, pulling on the jeans he had been wearing the previous day and the same shirt too.

"Mind if I join you? I would like to see my knight in action," Kyree chuckled, leading Ambrose down to the home gym, seeing Idella waiting on the mat.

"You're la-" Idella stopped abruptly when he saw Ambrose following Kyree.

"Sorry, Idella, I didn't want to wake your brother and I wasn't informed of any sort of schedule," Ambrose leant against the unpainted plain brick wall, propping one of his legs up as he flashed a small smirk to Kyree.

"Oh, it's fine, Your Majesty," Idella uttered quickly, his gaze dropping to the floor.

"Idella, please, call me Ambrose. There is no need for such formalities," Kyree chuckled, gaining a glare from his brother, he knew Idella hated how relaxed Kyree was with Ambrose. Then again, Idella hadn't been fucked by him.

"Can't you ever wear a shirt, Ky?" Idella frowned at his brother's bare chest, knowing all too well that Kyree rarely wore a full outfit when training. Kyree merely responded by kicking Idella's leg out from under him and knocking him onto the floor.

"Can't you ever put up a decent fight, little brother?" Kyree held out a hand to the scowling Idella, who batted it away and pulled himself to his feet by himself. When Idella's back hit the mat for the third time, Ambrose interrupted.

"Mind if I cut in, Idella?" he asked politely, pulling off his shirt. He was just about as muscular as Kyree, but his skin was much smoother, without the scars and bruising that came with daily training.

"Of course," Idella stumbled, moving off the mat quickly. Ambrose took his place, mischief glinting in his eyes as he smirked at Kyree. Kyree returned the smirk, expecting to win yet another easy fight. His overconfidence added to his surprise when his back hit the mat for the first time in a long time and all air was knocked from his lungs.

"What the..." Kyree marvelled up at Ambrose, who stood over him with a smug expression.

"Not used to losing then, are we?" Ambrose taunted as Kyree rose back to his feet. Idella was snickering to himself in the corner of the room, obviously very content with his brother being thrown around for once.

"Where did you learn to fight like that? I thought it was the job of your knight to learn that knowledge, not you," Ambrose shrugged as the two circled each other on the mat, each waiting for the other to make the first move.

"Can't hurt to be prepared, I didn't expect a knight as interesting as you so I trained myself with everything you learn," Kyree ducked before the fist Ambrose swung had chance to come into contact with his face, not realising he would just instead have Ambrose's foot hit his chest, sending stumbling backward coughing.

"Would you like me to go easier on you? You seem to be struggling," Ambrose teased, closing the distance between the two men. Kyree avoided two more punches and a kick from Ambrose, narrowly missing the demon's jaw as he swung a punch in turn.

"I'm not used to someone who actually knows how to fight, that's all, no offence little brother," Idella scoffed, rolling his eyes at Kyree's comment.

"You're the one getting your ass kicked now, don't bring my fighting skills into this," Ambrose took advantage of Kyree's guard dropping for simply a millisecond, his fist coming into contact with Kyree's perfect jaw, sending him stumbling backwards whilst the colours swam in his vision. Ambrose was pretty damn strong, Kyree was not used to that.

As Ambrose kicked Kyree's legs from under him and knocked him back onto the mat once again, he straddled his chest. Ambrose held down Kyree's arms easily, leaning in close with that smirk on his lips.

"Your lip is bleeding," he whispered, seduction laced into his cheeky tone. Before Kyree had a chance to respond, Ambrose's tongue darted out and licked away the drop of blood forming on Kyree's bottom lip, stunning the demon. Ambrose clearly took pleasure in making Kyree speechless, he did it often enough.

"Um, Ambrose?" Kyree's eyes flickered over to his father stood in the doorway of the gym, looking a little startled himself.

"Yes, Orion?" Ambrose sat up, still pinning Kyree to the mat, a much more appropriate expression of natural curiosity on his face.

"Osiris and Anubis seem to be growing restless without orders from you. As much as Yennifer loves having them help her around the house, I fear if she keeps them any longer she won't give them back to you," Kyree rubbed his wrists as Ambrose finally stood, smiling down at him then back at his father.

"I shall retrieve them now," the second Ambrose left the room, Orion's stern gaze focused on Kyree.

"He's engaged, Kyree, did you know that? Flirting with him is not an intelligent move now, is it?" Orion patronized Kyree constantly, acting as though he was still some immature teenager, not nearly 7 centuries old.

"A little flirting here and there causes no harm, father," Kyree retorted, rising to his feet so his father couldn't make him feel so inferior.

"Kyree," Orion stepped closer, much closer, "you will stop this nonsense right now. I'm not having the wrath of the Lord on this family. Ambrose being here is partially for your benefit too, you will distance yourself from His Majesty from now on, young man," Orion hissed, his dark green eyes intent on Kyree's hazel ones.

"I'm not a child any more father, you can't force me to-"

"In this house, you will obey my rules, Kyree. Don't talk back to me," his father growled, his voice much louder, silencing Kyree, "stay away from him, you understand?" Kyree scowled at his father, wishing he was as accepting as his mother, "Kyree! I asked, do you understand?"

"Yes! Yes, I fucking understand!" Kyree snapped, stalking out of the room, shouldering past a sheepish looking Idella along the way. Kyree's father didn't have a problem with Kyree liking men, he just clearly had a problem with Kyree 'tainting' Ambrose's reputation.

Kyree had many places up in the human world, various apartments and residents that he owned or rented. He left the underworld more often than even his brother knew about. He enjoyed watching the stars at night, hell didn't have stars. Down there, demons lived a starless existence, which was one of the things Kyree detested most about his home.

As he stood on the balcony of a more lavish condo that he owned, his gaze was set on the twinkling stars above. If he had been human, he would have picked astrophysics as his career path purely because he would get to star gaze. There was a cold breeze that night, sending chills down Kyree's spine.

As he turned to go and search for a hoodie to wear, he noticed a figure stood in the doorway watching him. His big build and crossed arms gave him away, despite Kyree not able to actually see his face.

"Go home, Ambrose, you're vulnerable up here, more so than at my father's mansion," Kyree muttered, venom in his tone at the mention of his father.

"Were you craving?" Ambrose said softly, stepping out of the shadows to stand in front of Kyree. They were both still shirtless and Kyree could feel hell's heat still radiating from Ambrose's bare skin.

"Do you see a human here?" Kyree grumbled, a little irritated by Ambrose's assumption that he had lost control.

"Why else would you be up here?"

"I like to watch the stars," Kyree shivered as Ambrose ran his warm fingertips up his forearm, then moved back out of his reach, "go home," Ambrose's face knotted into a soft frown, something Kyree found oddly pleasant to watch.

"Have I done something to upset you? Was it beating you on the mat? Or something else?" Kyree felt a twinge of pain shoot through his heart at Ambrose's concern. He forced his eyes away from the demon opposite him, choosing to stare at the moon illuminating them both from its position in the dark night sky.

"No."

"Ky," Ambrose coaxed, stepping closer and tilting Kyree's chin to face him, his grey-blue eyes filled with worry, "please, tell me what's wrong," Kyree sighed, both despising and admiring Ambrose's persistence.

"My father, he doesn't want me ruining your engagement. He doesn't want the wrath of your father on my family that would surely happen were I to steal you away from your rightful owner. I will just remain up here until you leave so as not to upset my father anymore," Ambrose clasped Kyree's fidgeting hands in his own, stilling Kyree's agitation.

"First, I'm not a possession to be owned, I am a person to be loved. Second, you know the situation with my fiance, your father has no right to ban you from being around me. I happen to enjoy your flirting a lot," Kyree could tell Ambrose was trying to insert some humour into the situation, but Kyree wasn't in the smiling mood.

"In my father's house, his rule is law," Kyree said simply, averting his eyes to the floor so Ambrose didn't have to frown upon the sorrow consuming his face.

"Is this also your father's house?"

"No, my father doesn't rent properties in the human world, he had no need."

"Then we stay here," Kyree looked up, catching Ambrose's smug gaze with his own bemused one, "this is your house, therefore no rules from your father, you can flirt with me all you like," Kyree tried very hard to suppress the smile he so desperately wanted to express, thoughts more crucial than his own selfish feelings taking precedence in his mind.

"You're vulnerable up here, Ambrose, I'm not worth taking that risk," Ambrose's grin only grew as the two men from the foyer appeared behind him.

"You've already met Anubis and Osiris, my personal guards until I get my knight, that is. They will ensure I am safe if you're not feeling up to the job that is," the notion wasn't terrible, but Kyree knew there were too many holes in Ambrose's plan to remain in the human world.

"How long would we stay? My father will send people after you the minute he knows you're gone. We wouldn't even last a month up here, if it weren't my father it would be humans. We don't fit here," Ambrose nodded curtly toward Osiris and Anubis, who ventured inside probably to secure the apartment and maybe even the whole building.

"You managed to do so when you came here so often. I'm sure I could learn."

Chapter 7

Kyree realised very quickly that arguing with Ambrose was pointless, he just wouldn't give in. He could see the links between Ambrose and the Lord easily when he acted this way, never giving up until he got his way.

"Where did you learn how to cook?" Ambrose's voice drifted over the soft music playing from the stereo sat on the countertop in the corner of the kitchen.

"Alexander taught me, he didn't want the chance that I would poison him," a ghost of a smile worked its way onto Kyree's dark lips as he continued to slice away at the slab of raw red meat on the chopping board. Out of the corner of his eye, Kyree could just about see Anubis watching him cook with a frown on his face.

"I'm not going to poison Ambrose, Anubis, don't worry. I'm not stupid enough to do it with the both of you around," Kyree referenced Osiris but he wasn't entirely sure where the other demon guard had gone to. As Kyree slid the pieces of meat into the sizzling frying pan, he felt the familiar sensation of Ambrose's warm fingers grazing over his bare hips. With the condo being particularly warm inside compared to the balcony,

Kyree opted to leave his shirt off, knowing he would feel no pain if oil spilt onto his skin. He had hellfire in his veins, nothing could burn him.

"What are you doing?" Kyree asked softly, suppressing the growl of pleasure that threatened to leave his lips. Ambrose's chest brushing against Kyree's bare back as his fingers trailed around to his abs reminded him of their first night together, awakening a yearning for more than he could not possibly act on.

"Helping," Ambrose rested his chin on Kyree's broad shoulder, stroking his hands down Kyree's forearms, resting his hands over his.

"More like seducing," Kyree whispered, trying unsuccessfully to keep his focus on the meat cooking in the pan. He didn't want to overcook the steaks, it wasn't that they were expensive, he just wanted to impress Ambrose.

"Maybe, I lost my appetite anyway, for food that is," Ambrose's fingers rested on the worn leather belt, just skimming the gold metal of the buckle. Kyree wanted to melt back into Ambrose's arms, to feel the pleasure he had felt that first night. Yet he knew he couldn't, being with a man who was engaged didn't feel right, even if Ambrose wasn't interested in his fiance, Kyree had brought up to know better.

"Ambrose," Kyree said softly, shifting his hips slightly in the hopes Ambrose would grasp his apprehension, "stop," Ambrose's lips left a trail of fire in their path along Kyree's neck. It was getting more and more difficult to resist Ambrose's advances, but the rage from his father instantly sobered Kyree.

"Stop," Kyree said, his tone more forceful as he removed Ambrose's hands from his hips and moved out of his grasp. Ambrose's dark eyes instantly flared with worry in their grey-blue mixture.

"Did I do something wrong?" he asked, his voice much quieter, a soft frown on his face, "Ky, you gotta tell me if I'm pushing you too far. I can't read minds, y'know," Kyree sighed, not really sure how to explain his discomfort. He wanted Ambrose, in every way, yet he knew he couldn't have him. Kyree still had feelings for Alexander and, despite so desperately wanting to experiment more with whatever he had with Ambrose, he saw himself as dangerous. The last thing he wanted to do was hurt Ambrose again, he didn't think he could deal with the guilt for a second time.

"I gotta make these steaks," Kyree merely grumbled, slumping in front of the cooker again, ensuring his back was to Ambrose so he didn't have to see his bemused expression.

"Is this about what your father said?" Ambrose knew Kyree better than he knew himself, yet he had always had a knack for reading people anyway, "because he had no right to say any of it. He doesn't know the full story, he probably wouldn't care if I told him. He seems to be a stubborn, old man intent on ruining your happiness for you. I'm not letting that happen," Kyree remained silent, he had hurt Ambrose enough, speaking would only worsen the effect, "Ky, fucking talk to me. Is this about your father or not?"

"I don't know, Amb! OK? I don't fucking know!" Kyree hung his head after his outburst, his hands gripping the countertop so hard his knuckles turned white. He didn't want to lose his temper, he couldn't, not with Ambrose anywhere close enough to be caught in the crossfire.

"Ky, please, talk to me," Ambrose rubbed small circles over Kyree's tense shoulders, hoping to aid in relaxing him in some way.

"I told you before, Amb, I don't know how to be with someone anymore. What happened with Alexander broke me, ripped me into so many pieces I'm not sure where to start. I feel... something for you, I just don't know what it is. I'm a danger. I hurt you once, with my temper it's bound to happen again. It's not a question of if, it's when," Kyree felt defeated, weary even.

"Let me help put you back together then," Ambrose said softly, turning Kyree to face him, "I told you before, I just want to help you. Even if you don't want to be with me, I want to help give you the happiness you once had. Tonight, I took it too far and I apologise. I won't try anything until you're better, OK?" Kyree stared up into those beautiful grey-blue eyes, filled with so much empathy for a demon.

"It's not fair for you, Amb, you deserve-"

"What you think I deserve isn't important right now, your sanity is on the line, don't let it snap," Ambrose's lips curled into a faint smile, igniting a warm fuzzy feeling in Kyree's chest.

"OK," Kyree whispered, wrapping his arms around Ambrose's waist and resting his head on his firm chest, "I would like that," the two men remained in that position for a short while, Ambrose cradling Kyree as though he was a child. That was, until Kyree smelt the burning meat.

"Fuck," Kyree sighed, staring down at the blackened steaks in the pan. Ambrose stood close behind Kyree, examining the damage from over his shoulder yet making sure not to overstep his boundaries.

"I'm honestly not that hungry, Ky," Ambrose reassured Kyree as he threw out the steaks, his brows drawn together in a frown.

"Yeah, OK, maybe we'll just order something in a little later. I clearly overstated my cooking skills, you are very distracting," Kyree's confident personality had returned, that glint in his eye twinkling as he glanced toward Ambrose.

"It's nearly midnight, y'know, Ky, maybe we should just go to bed," Ambrose offered, a smile on his lips. Kyree desperately wanted to be held by

Ambrose again, to feel the slumber so deep he wouldn't feel tired for days. Yet he wasn't sure if Ambrose meant going to bed together, and he didn't want to force it on him. It still felt odd to him to have to merely sleep with another man in his bed also.

"OK," Kyree strode over to the couch, moving the pillows to one side and unfurling a blanket over it.

"Ky, you expect us both to fit on there? Is there not a bedroom in this place?" Ambrose said, adding a soft chuckle when he saw Kyree looking a little flustered.

"I didn't know if you wanted to- or whether-" Ambrose merely clasped Kyree's hand, following his directions to the bedroom.

"I told you, until you're better I'm your bed buddy," Ambrose stripped down to just his boxers, laying in the large bed and awaiting Kyree to join him. Kyree mirrored Ambrose's actions, laying down next to him and rolling onto his side with his back to Ambrose. Before Kyree had time to remember that Ambrose was comfortable holding him, he felt the demon's arm snake around and rest on his waist.

"Goodnight, Ky," Ambrose whispered, his chest pressed against Kyree's back as he left a short but sweet kiss on Kyree's smooth cheek.

"Goodnight, Amb," Kyree replied, drifting out of consciousness almost immediately, however, not into the peaceful slumber he had yearned for...

"Where is he? He's late," Kyree pushed through the thick crowd of people, scanning every face in search of his lover. He wasn't there. He was almost 20 minutes late and guests were getting restless.

"Father!" Kyree called out as he saw Orion stood with his mother, "father, have you seen him?" panic was rising in Kyree, his heart almost beating out of his chest, sorrow building within him.

"No, son, I'm so sorry," Orion patted his son's shoulder, a gesture that was all he could really do at that time. His mother had a much more sympathetic look on her face, a soft frown of pain knotting her brows.

"Oh, Ky, you didn't deserve this. I thought he truly loved you," Yennifer cupped her child's cheeks, hoping her affection could make up some small part of what he lost with his lover.

"He does love me, mother, have some faith," Kyree snapped, stepping back out of his mother's reach, sick of everyone thinking his lover had left him, "I have to find him, he must have lost track of time," Kyree sped off again, shouldering through the guests who had exited their seats as their patience ran dry, ignoring their tutting and complaining about his rudeness.

"Idella!" Kyree's brother was leaning against the stone wall of the church, his eyes on the ground, "Idella, brother, please tell me you've seen him," Idella had a look of guilt on his face too, but who didn't by that time.

"He went to the human world, Ky, he told me it was to get a surprise for you. Your favourite flowers to put in your suit pocket, I didn't think he would-" Kyree had disappeared before he had chance to hear the rest, appearing under a large oak tree.

Kyree and his lover visited that place often, the cool breeze drifting from the nearby coastline making the air have a salty scent to it. That morning was bright, the sun almost blinding Kyree, forcing him to squint his eyes as he scanned the area for his lover.

There was a figure stood under the oak tree, their body casting a shadow back toward where Kyree was stood. In fact, they looked almost... no, that couldn't be. They looked like they were floating, their feet not quite touching the ground. As Kyree's eyes finally adjusted to the light, he felt as though all the air had been knocked from his lungs. The figure wasn't floating... it was hanging.

"No, no, no," Kyree ran toward the figure, stumbling in the long grass as tears stung his eyes. It couldn't be.

"Please, no, no, no," Kyree begged as he finally saw the face of the corpse. His world rocked, tipped, fell and shattered into a million pieces. His legs gave way beneath him as he stared into the eyes of his lover and he crumbled to the floor, tears streaming down his cheeks. He wanted to shout, scream, kill. But he just couldn't break his gaze from those eyes that had once been such a vibrant grey-blue yet had faded to a dull almost black.

"No, no, no," Kyree sobbed, his whole body trembling with grief and anger, "please, baby, not you," he whimpered, "please, open your eyes, baby. I can't lose you..."

Kyree awoke abruptly, a sharp gasp all he could manage before his emotions kicked him in the stomach and he fell into hysterics. His entire body shook as he sat up in bed, every muscle rigid in his form. It wasn't long before tears fell over the rim of Kyree's eyes, fear consuming him as he took large, broken breaths.

"Ky, calm down, it's OK, you're OK," Kyree felt Ambrose's sat up awfully close next to him, tugging him into his chest, "it was a dream, Ky, just a dream," Kyree allowed Ambrose to hold him, sobbing softly into his chest. Kyree had had that dream before, yet it had never been so vivid, never felt so real.

"It was- God, I never-" Kyree couldn't finish a sentence, the words jumbling up as they spilt over his lips, hysterics taking control in his mind.

"I know, baby, I know. It's OK, you're OK now," Ambrose pressed kisses into Kyree's mess of brunette locks, holding his trembling body against his own. He too was wracked with worry, his mind moving in overdrive as he tried to process what had just happened. In Kyree's state, Ambrose didn't want to worry him further by confiding that he had woken up seconds earlier from the exact same dream...

Chapter 8

Kyree was awoken by something licking his cheek and hot breath on his face. He grimaced, a soft groan slipping out of his mouth as it curved into a smile.

"Amb, this is so not a sexy way to wake someone up," Kyree muttered groggily, rubbing his heavy eyes.

"As hilarious as it would be to wake you up this way, it's not me," Ambrose remarked from across the room, leaning in the doorway to the bedroom. Kyree opened his eyes slowly, then a melodic laugh trickled from his mouth.

"Endwin," Kyree beamed at the dark coloured animal sat on the bed in Ambrose's place, "you brought my dog here? What are you buttering me up for?" Kyree asked, ruffling the fur on Endwin's head as it rested on his lap. Ambrose smiled innocently, gazing around the room.

"What on earth would make you think that? I just thought you would like your dog up here with us," Kyree cocked an eyebrow, causing Ambrose to chuckle, "OK, I may have something I would like to talk to you about," Ambrose perched on the bed, stroking his hand up over Kyree's leg gingerly.

"What would you like to talk to me about then?" Kyree said after a few seconds of Ambrose merely staring at his hand resting on Kyree's thigh. Ambrose blinked a few times, rousing himself from whatever daydream he had drifted into.

"That dream you had, a few nights ago," Kyree sighed at the mention of that Goddamn nightmare, when it wasn't haunting him in his mind Ambrose was pestering him about it, "I was waiting until you opened up to me about it to tell you this, but at this rate I don't think I would get to tell you this century," Ambrose paused for a second, simpering when he noticed Kyree still staring at him, "I had the same dream.""What? What are you talking about?" Kyree sat up, far more intrigued by Ambrose's little confession than he thought he would be.

"I woke up seconds before you. I had the same dream. I know exactly what it was. I wanted to make sure before I told you but you refused to open up," Kyree frowned, deep in thought.

"I've never heard of anything like this before, you're sure it was my dream? How do you even know if you don't know what my dream was?" Ambrose expected denial, he had been focused on the stupid nightmare for days.

"It's difficult to explain. I wasn't in a body in the dream, more like in spirit. I followed you, just watching. But I woke up just before I could see his face, who was it, Ky? Who was hanging?" Kyree grimaced, the image from that nightmare truly would be burnt into his brain for the rest of eternity, "was it Alexander?"

"No," Kyree said softly, locking his worried gaze with Ambrose's, "it was you," shocked, Ambrose was silent, his eyes a little wider than before, "I need to take Endwin for a walk, do you want to join me?" Kyree asked as he rose to his feet, his muscles rippling as he stretched his arms above his head.

"Yeah, sure," Ambrose said, but his voice was distant. Kyree bent down in front of him, caressing his cheek with his thumb.

"Hey," Kyree coaxed Ambrose to look at him with his beautiful grey-blue eyes, "whatever this is, whatever is going on between us, we're gonna figure this out, OK?" Ambrose nodded weakly, yet Kyree was not satisfied, "Amb, we're OK. This shit isn't normal but neither of us are dying, OK? We're gonna be fine," when Ambrose's lips finally curved into a small smile, Kyree stood, pressing a chaste kiss on Ambrose's forehead along the way. Kyree threw on a pair of black jeans and a white t-shirt, not bothering to collect a jacket on his way out with it being relatively tepid outside.

With one hand clasped in Ambrose's and the other holding Endwin's leash, Kyree led the way to a nearby park. For some reason, the fact that he had shared a dream with Ambrose didn't affect him as much as really it should have. Then again, sharing a dream was much less daunting than what he had been through in his life.

"I see now why you like to come up here so often," Ambrose smirked, eyeing a couple of men who walked past shirtless as Kyree threw a stick for Endwin. Kyree chuckled, glancing at the men then at Ambrose.

"I've seen better, I'm looking at better right now," with Kyree in a seemingly good mood, Ambrose couldn't resist wrapping his arms around his waist. Kyree's back fit so well against Ambrose's chest as if they were moulded to go together like pieces of a puzzle.

"Who would have thought I would be stood in the human world, holding a demon and throwing a stick for a dog? It's amazingly domestic," Ambrose's breath tickled Kyree's ear, causing his grin to widen. Kyree rested his hands over Ambrose's, kissing his cheek as he felt his chin rest on his shoulder.

"Too domestic for the prince of hell?" Kyree responded, keeping his voice low to ensure no passing humans caught any of their conversation.

"No, I think I quite like it up here. I do often wonder why we are no longer allowed to roam freely on this plane," Ambrose let go of Kyree for a second, leaning down to throw the stick for Endwin then returning to his position immediately.

"Because of what happened to Alexander," Kyree's voice didn't falter, although he still felt the gentle tug of pain when Alexander's name touched his lips. He was getting better, which pleased him.

"Really?"

"I assume so. It was only a few days after Alexander's death that your father announced the ban and there were no other acts as heinous around that time," sadness swirled in Ambrose as he opened his mouth to say something, "please, I'm OK, you don't need to make any sort of apology about it. Being around you up here has helped significantly. At least I don't start throwing punches the minute anyone mentions his name," a compassionate smile spread over Ambrose's face as he tightened his grip on Kyree, pressing a few kisses on his shoulder.

Scoffs and loud grumbling nearby ruined the moment between Kyree and Ambrose. Two other men around the same age as Kyree looked were scowling at Ambrose embracing Kyree, disgust plastered across their faces.

"Scum," one of them spat, igniting an anger in Kyree that he hadn't felt since Alexander was alive. Anger fuelled by the discrimination of who he chose to love.

"What did you say?" Kyree growled, glaring right back at the men, fixed in his place by Ambrose's strong grip.

"I said, fuckin' scum," the taller man who had spoken before repeated, venom in his tone, "you're sinnin', lyin' with another man, it's fuckin' disgustin'," the man grunted, his thick accent revealing Southern American ties in his bloodline. Kyree's blood was boiling, every fibre in his body screaming at him to rip the two men apart, but he was in public, it would reveal what he was.

"I advise walking away, whilst your legs are still attached to your body," Kyree threatened, the sensation of Ambrose's hands on his hips the only thing keeping him grounded at that moment. Fear flickered across the men's faces as a low snarl rippled through the peaceful atmosphere of the park. Kyree knew it was Edwin and he so desperately wanted to allow his hellhound to attack. But he knew that soon enough Endwin would grow to be the size of a grizzly bear and there would be no explanation for that.

"Endwin, down," Kyree commanded, a glimmer of pride crossing his face as Endwin instantly sat, silent.

"That mutt should be on a Goddamn leash," the other, smaller man spoke that time, venom also in his tone, but more so directed at Endwin.

"I thought I told you to leave. If you find us so disgraceful to your backwards ideologies then go elsewhere," Kyree snapped, drawing the attention back to Ambrose and himself.

"It's you two that should leave. We don't except scum like you around these parts," the taller man spoke again, if you could call his string of grunts and growls speech. Ambrose had loosened his grip for just a second, giving Kyree the chance to slip out of it. And out came Kyree's anger. An anger, a beast, that hadn't risen from its slumber for almost half a decade.

Kyree didn't even realise what he had done until it was too late. By the time the clouds of fury rolled away from his eyes, both men were lying limp on the grass. Kyree was knelt on the taller man's chest and he could feel the shattered ribs under his knees. Blood was everywhere. Spattered on Kyree's face, his knuckles, across his white shirt.

"Ky," Ambrose was at his side in an instant, holding him as he stared at his dirty work, "they deserved it, Ky, they weren't innocent. They're alive, you didn't kill them. But you sure as hell taught them a lesson. It's OK, let's go home," Ambrose helped Kyree to his feet, cupping his cheeks, "Kyree, don't you dare feel bad for this. First, you're a demon, you have every right to want to kill, to have an uncontrollable anger that you let out every so often. Second, people like those men are not the ones you should be feeling remorse for. It was self-defence, OK, they provoked you. Come on, we need to get home before someone sees something."

For hours, Kyree simply laid and stared at the ceiling in his bedroom. His anger was growing, despite thinking he was getting better, nothing changed regarding Kyree's temper. He was a timebomb.

"Ky," Ambrose's soft voice soothed Kyree, yet he still remained still, "Ky, I think we should go back down to the underworld," Kyree's gazed snapped to Ambrose stood in the doorway, a frown mirroring his.

"What? Why? You were the one that wanted to stay up here, why go back now?" Kyree sat up, sighing, "whatever, Ambrose, go back then. But I'm staying up here, I still don't want to anger my father," Kyree hung his head in his hands, so many thoughts rushing through his mind. Ambrose knelt in front of Kyree, resting his hands on Kyree's knees gently.

"Ky, please come back with me, I don't like the thought of leaving you up here alone," with every word that Ambrose spoke, Kyree felt a part of him relax, Ambrose truly could tame his anger.

"What's the point? I'll just hurt you, or my father will kick me out for flirting with you or-" Kyree was silenced by Ambrose's mouth covering his. It was gentle, soft, something Kyree didn't often experience. He responded instantly, lacing his fingers into Ambrose's hair and tugging him closer, wanting to feel more and more.

Suddenly a sharp pain jolted through Kyree's back, gradually flowing through his chest. His movements ceased, catching Ambrose's attention too, the pain growing to an insurmountable sensation. He could barely breathe, all air knocked from his lungs.

"Fuck, Kyree, oh my God," Ambrose gasped as he pulled away and saw the blood seeping through Kyree's already ruined white shirt. Kyree stared at him with worry in his eyes, his grip on Ambrose's arms being the only thing holding him upright.

Osiris and Anubis joined Ambrose, helping him lower Kyree to the ground as he whispered over and over that he was gonna be OK. The metallic taste of blood had already invaded his mouth and his vision was beginning to cloud. He wasn't so sure Ambrose was right.

"S-Sorry..." Kyree managed to choke out, just as the lights flickered off in his mind.

Chapter 9

When Kyree managed to force his eyes open, he was no longer in the condo with Ambrose and his guards. In fact, he had no idea where he was. His gaze scanned the area, searching for any discernible features. None. Nothing. He was still unsure of where he had appeared.

"Ambrose?" Kyree called out, his voice echoing through the stagnant air. Wind whipped around him on the cliff edge, blanketing him in the cold. The sea battered the rocks below, it's movements aggressive, reminding Kyree of his own nature.

"Hello, Kyree," that voice, Kyree knew that voice, that was the one voice that made his heart stop with every word. A voice he never thought he would get to hear again. He didn't dare look toward the origin of the voice, didn't want the source to disappear.

"It's OK, bunny," a twinge of sorrow struck Kyree, he hadn't been called bunny for a long time, "you can look at me," slowly he turned his head, attempting to blink away the tears welling in his eyes. He didn't manage to quell all the tears, for one did fall when he saw a face he had so dearly missed. His sandy brown hair falling out of place over his pale, freckled face, almost covering those piercing green eyes.

"Oh, bunny," his brows drew into a frown, something Kyree had always found adorable.

"Alexander?" Kyree whispered, his lip quivering as he tried so desperately to contain the waterfall of emotions consuming him.

"Who else would it be, bunny?" as Alexander smiled that beautiful smile, Kyree broke down, tears trickling down his cheeks at a steady pace, "hey, stop crying. What happened to my big, bad, scary demon?" Alexander cupped Kyree's cheeks, wiping away the tears with his thumbs. Kyree instantly gripped Alexander's waist, pulling him flush against his body as he buried his face in his shoulder, inhaling that musty, flowery scent.

"Bunny, you gotta get a hold of yourself," Alexander spoke cheerfully, his hand absently trailing through Kyree's brunette locks, "I don't want you wasting the rest of your life missing me," Kyree chuckled bitterly, lifting his head to see those beautiful eyes again.

"What life, Lex? If you're here, I'm clearly dead."

"You're not dead, bunny," Alexander's lips dropped to a less vibrant smile, a softer one, more compassionate, "dying, maybe, but not dead. And you're not gonna die for a long while, you're needed for something very important. You and that prince," at the mention of Ambrose, Kyree suddenly felt very conflicted, "he's very handsome, you always did pick attractive men, bunny. You like him, don't you?" Kyree shrugged, averting his eyes to the ground, "you're allowed to like him. It's not cheating, I'm dead."

"I don't know, Lex, after what happened to you, I don't really remember much about love," Alexander lifted Kyree's head, forcing him to make eye contact.

"Of course you do, bunny, give yourself some credit. You always were an amazing lover. You're kind, compassionate, great in bed. You haven't lost the ability to do any of that, bunny, it might just be a little muddled up in that mind of yours."

"Lex, I don't wanna hurt him.""Bunny, you lost control once, OK? Once. Let him into your heart, let go of me. You deserve happiness and that prince can give it to you. If anyone can tame you, it's him," the sun illuminating the two men began to grow, almost blinding Kyree, "we're out of time, bunny, remember I love you. Stop loving me and give that prince a chance," panic swelled in Kyree as he felt the cliff receding behind him, huge chunks of rock falling into the sea below.

"I don't wanna leave you, Lex, please, let me stay," Alexander chuckled softly, the sound washing away all pain in Kyree.

"Bunny, you can't stay here. You have a prince to get back to. Keep dreaming about me, just not my death," Alexander pressed a soft kiss on Kyree's lips just as the rock behind him crumbled. Kyree tried to grasp Alexander's shirt, but his hands merely slipped through it and he fell.

As he experienced the weightlessness, the force of the wind, Kyree held onto Alexander's words. He had to move on. He was no longer Alexander's, he yearned to be Ambrose's...

The sensation of a small piece of metal ripping through flesh is a difficult one to explain. Kyree had always thought it didn't look that painful. He was wrong. The pain was intense, a dull stabbing ache that somehow increased with every breath.

"Mrs Landon, please, lower your voice, I don't want him woken," Kyree heard Ambrose's voice first, a faint smile tugging at his lips.

"I don't care if you're a prince, I don't care if you're to be a king, do not tell me how to act in front of my son! Who you got shot!" Yennifer was shrieking, a piercing sound that simply added to the ache flowing through

Kyree's body. So he was back in the underworld, wonderful, he couldn't wait to be yelled at by his father for stealing the prince for mere days.

"Mother..." Kyree forced out, his mouth dry, his eyes only able to open slightly.

"Kyree," Yennifer's voice was much closer, and thankfully, much softer, "oh, Kyree, my baby, how are you?" Kyree tried his best to focus on Yennifer, but his eyes simply yearned to stare at Ambrose, stood across the room with a deep frown on his face.

"It's not Ambrose's fault," Kyree's voice was raspy, yet his mother heard every word clearly.

"He got you shot, Kyree, it is his fault," Kyree glared at his mother, or tried to anyway.

"What happened to 'it's only your fault if you pulled the trigger'?" Kyree quoted something his mother had told him a lot when Alexander had died, perfectly content to use her own words against her.

"Well, Kyree this is diff-"

"No, it's not," Kyree interrupted, reaching out his hand to Ambrose, despite only lifting it a few centimetres from the bed he was laid on, "Amb," he whispered, weakly. Ambrose was at his side in an instant, knelt down so he was at eye level, clasping Kyree's hand in his own.

"I'm here, Ky, what is it?" Ambrose looked tired, worry swirling in his grey-blue eyes.

"Pretty shit first kiss, huh?" Ambrose's face warmed with a smile, as he pressed a few chaste kisses to Kyree's hand.

"Actually, that wasn't our first kiss, if you remember correctly," a smirk tugged lazily at the corners of Kyree's mouth as he remembered that night.

"I thought you wanted to forget that night, you said it ruin us both," Kyree noticed Yennifer looking suspicious and decided it was time she knew how he had met Ambrose, "mother, I met Ambrose the night before he came to dinner. In the human world. Isn't that ironic? Two demon men meeting in a bar, both assuming the other is human," the frown on Yennifer's face grew, "mother, I'm safe with Ambrose, please leave us so I can sleep," Kyree didn't have the energy to explain in further detail what had happened during that night to his mother, she understood the basics, which was what Kyree had wanted. Yennifer, for once, respected Kyree's wishes and left him alone with Ambrose.

"So, your assassin doesn't seem a great shot if he hit me instead of you," Kyree uttered, grimacing as he shifted a little in bed. Ambrose looked glum, guilt in his eyes instead of worry.

"Kyree, you don't understand how awful I feel-"

"Don't. I meant what I said when it wasn't your fault, don't blame yourself for something you couldn't control. Trust me, I know it doesn't help," Kyree gingerly ran his fingertips down Ambrose's cheek, a faint smile on his face, "come lay with me, I sleep better with you," Ambrose rose to his feet and strode around to the other side of the bed. Removing his shirt, he laid down next to Kyree and carefully helped him lay half on his bare chest. Kyree glanced down at the large bandage wrapped around his torso, another scar and another story to tell.

"Alexander called you bunny?" Ambrose teased, a smirk in his tone and on his face, "doesn't really suit your personality, Ky," Kyree chuckled softly, lifting his head to catch Ambrose's eye.

"Really? You even get to snoop in on my death dreams? This is not fair, won't I ever get to see any of yours?"

"Apparently not," Ambrose stroked his hand down Kyree's back, avoiding the bandage, "how do you feel after seeing him?" Ambrose's tone was soft yet serious, not wanting to provoke Kyree.

"Better, I think I needed it. At least now my final memory of him isn't his death," the two were silent for a short while, Kyree knew Ambrose was wanting to ask a certain question but didn't know how to word it.

"Are you going to..." Ambrose trailed off, sighing and looking away.

"Listen to what he said? Give you a chance? Let you tame me?" Kyree smiled, tilting Ambrose's head so he could press a soft kiss to his lips, "what do you think?"

Chapter 10

"I just don't think it's a very good idea," Kyree grumbled, wincing as he crossed his arms over his chest. It was only three days after Kyree had been shot and his wound still ached. The bullet had been laced with devil's snare to slow down Kyree's healing, it must have or he wouldn't still be in so much pain.

"Kyree, we have to act normal or people will get suspicious. This is what we would do if Ambrose wasn't here so we have to," Orion frowned as Ambrose exited Kyree's ensuite with just a towel around his waist, his dark locks dripping and his bare chest glistening in the lights. He still did not like the two together, not with Ambrose engaged, but he knew he had no right to get between them.

"Amb, please tell me you're not OK with this stupid idea," Ambrose chuckled, pushing his hair out of his face as he perched on the bed next to Kyree and opposite Orion, careful to keep the towel tight around his bare form.

"I have my knight, Anubis and Osiris. I feel perfectly safe, go ahead with it, have no objections," Kyree glared at him, batting Ambrose's hand away when he tried to clasp it around Kyree's.

"Agree with me or I'm not sucking your cock for a week," Kyree threatened, simply causing Ambrose to laugh as he rose back to his feet.

"Don't pout, Ky, it's immature," Ambrose slipped into a pair of black sweatpants, ensuring Orion didn't see anything he didn't need to.

"God, you're all idiots, y'know that?" Kyree said, exasperation laced into his tone, "I got shot three days ago, what's to stop the fucking assassin trying again so soon after? He found Ambrose up in the human world, he can easily find him down here. I don't need a masked ball for my birthday, OK? I don't even want one. It would just be an easy way to get Ambrose killed."

"Kyree, we throw a ball every year for your birthday, just because you didn't even attend the last 4 does not mean we aren't throwing you one this year. We have to act normal, like I have already told you multiple times," Kyree merely rolled his eyes at his father's flawed logic.

"Whatever," he muttered as his father exited the room, after informing him he had to be ready in an hour, or else.

"Ky, I'm gonna be fine," Ambrose reassured as Kyree stood slowly, holding his torso with a grimace on his face.

"You better be, you're not leaving my side all night, OK? I don't care if you feel safe with Osiris and Anubis too, just stay with me," Ambrose smiled at Kyree's overprotective nature, "I mean it, Amb."

"I know, baby, I will," satisfied, Kyree grasped Ambrose's waist and pulled him flush against his chest despite the pain, their lips crashing together. Ambrose groaned softly, one hand draped around the back of Kyree's neck, the other caressing his cheek. Kyree loved the feeling of Ambrose's lips on his, craved it almost every moment of the day.

He knew at the stupid event his parents were throwing for him he would not be able to show his affection toward Ambrose, not even with him wearing a mask. It would be too risky, too many questions would be asked. Although it would instir that awful empty feeling in the both of them, it would be easier to just act as acquaintances.

"Mmm, you should really be getting dressed, baby, not distracting me," Ambrose half scolded, his lips so close they still brushed against Kyree's, sending shivers down his spine.

"Or we could get undressed and try again in half an hour?" Kyree smirked, trailing his fingertip across the sweatpant waistband hugging Ambrose's hips loosely. Ambrose chuckled, cutting off all physical contact as he stepped back out of Kyree's reach.

"Maybe tonight, baby, if you behave," Ambrose teased, turning away and opening the closet. He had moved most of his clothes into Kyree's room since they slept together, it made everything a whole lot easier. Kyree observed as Ambrose tugged off the sweatpants. Kyree's lip caught between his teeth, he knew his eyes had darkened as he watched his God-like demon undress.

"Now what did I do to deserve such a hot piece of ass?" his voice was low, husky with lust, his eyes fixed on Ambrose's bare form. He truly was built like a God, his muscles well defined, his skin tanned and smooth, and his ass... God, Kyree could spend a thousand years merely staring at Ambrose's ass.

"I will make you take a cold shower, Kyree Landon, I do not have time to suck your cock right now, neither of us do," Ambrose threatened, a cheeky smile on his lips as he dressed into his all-black suit, pairing it with a red tie as he had the night he had first entered the Landon mansion.

"You're the one stripping in front of me," Kyree retorted, smiling as he dressed in black slacks and a steel grey shirt paired with a maroon blazer.

Due to Kyree's injury, Ambrose had to help put his black tie on, giving him the chance run his hands over Ambrose's hips, a smirk on his lips.

"You're so fucking beautiful," Kyree muttered as his eyes flickered over Ambrose's face, inciting a flush of colour in his cheeks.

"Shut it," he murmured, pushing back a lock of Kyree's hair that had fallen out of place.

"You are, Amb," Ambrose simpered as he put Kyree's mask on him. It was a deep burgundy, with black lace and silver inlaid across it. Ambrose put on his own mask, a black one with golden inlay, that almost perfectly matched Kyree's.

Judging by the increasing noise drifting from downstairs, Kyree assumed many guests were already there. Ambrose and Kyree strolled downstairs, nodding curtly toward Idella when they passed him. A sudden burst of panic swelled within Kyree as it finally hit him that he would be at one of his parent's events for the first time in half a decade.

"Hey," Ambrose said softly, "it's gonna be fine, baby," Kyree didn't have chance to respond before the doors to the ballroom swung open and all eyes landed on the two men. Naturally, Kyree froze up as the room fell silent, everyone shocked to see Kyree make an appearance, despite it being an event thrown for him.

Just as Kyree regained control of his body and made the move to walk back upstairs, Ambrose pulled his head toward him, kissing him. A wave of gasps was the only noise the guests made, completely unaware that it was the prince of hell locking lips with Kyree.

The fear was drowned by the overwhelming sense of unity Kyree felt, his body alight with happiness in that one moment. Wanting to keep the kiss short and allow the night to continue on, Ambrose pulled away, slipping his hand into Kyree's.

"Kyree," Orion's voice echoed through the room as he engulfed him in a gentle hug, "name, quickly," he said in a tone so quiet only Kyree could hear.

"Antuon Walker," Kyree whispered into his father's ear as he returned the hug graciously, a little irritated he had to cut contact from Ambrose. Orion released Kyree from the hug, standing next to him with his hand on his son's back.

"Many of you weren't expecting Kyree to make an appearance tonight, judging by the shocked expressions," Orion began, the smile of a proud father on his lips, in fact, over his entire face. There was not a hint of anger for his son's display of affection with Ambrose, maybe his father was truly warming up to the idea of them being together.

"I will not lie to you all, Kyree has struggled with the tragic event that struck us almost 5 years ago," Kyree gripped Ambrose's hand once again, yearning for the sense of relief he felt with they made physical contact, "however, with the help of his family and friends, he has regained the happiness he once had with another, Antuon Walker," Orion turned his attention to Kyree and Ambrose, surprising Kyree with his watery eyes, "I'm so proud of you, Kyree, and so happy to welcome Antuon into the family. Happy birthday, my boy."

Chapter 11

It didn't take long for people to resume what they had been before Kyree and Ambrose had entered the room. Yennifer gushed over how Kyree and Ambrose looked together, hugging Kyree just a little too tight then apologising profusely. As Kyree and Ambrose lingered on the edges of the room, Kyree intent on talking to as little people as possible, he noticed Tyrell stood with Orion and Yennifer.

"Fucking bastard," Kyree seethed, the colour seeping from his eyes. Ambrose took ahold of his hands, not giving him a chance to go near Tyrell.

"Ky, baby, not here, not now," Ambrose spoke softly, his voice relaxing Kyree as he rubbed his thumbs across his knuckles. Kyree inhaled deeply, the colour returning to his eyes.

"I want him gone, I told him I would kill him if I saw him on this property again," Kyree growled, allowing his tension to flow away as his mind was lost in the sensation of Ambrose's touch.

"Then he's gone, baby," Ambrose nodded curtly toward Anubis but he wasn't fast enough. Orion had already directed Tyrell over to Kyree and Ambrose, believing he was only helping out.

"Kyree, happy birthday," Tyrell said in a sickly sweet voice, "I see you've finally moved on from my brother then, lucky you," once again, Kyree's eyes darkened to black, his hands clenched into fists.

"Get out," Kyree snarled, feeling his control slipping with each second Tyrell was in his sight.

"Kyree, I came to wish you a happy birthday, you're not acting like a very good host. Alexander would be disappointed," Kyree was about to snap, but Ambrose beat him to it.

"Out!" Ambrose boomed, his reserved nature clearly taken over by his demonic one, "this is your last fucking warning you pathetic piece of shit. You are not welcome here. Kyree is getting better, he is getting past Alexander's death and you do not need to come here and rub salt into his fucking wounds," even Kyree looked a little shocked at Ambrose's outburst, which had obviously caught the attention of every guest in the room.

"You have no right to speak to me like that," Tyrell shot back, fury and a hint of embarrassment on his face.

"When you're making my boyfriend uncomfortable, I have every fucking right. Get out, before I have you thrown out," Kyree was speechless, although he did look a little smug as Tyrell scurried from the room, his cheeks heating as everyone stared, "I need some air," Ambrose muttered, stalking out of the room mere seconds after Tyrell.

"Staring is fucking rude, go back to your drinks," Kyree snapped, following Ambrose out. Ambrose was surprisingly fast, Kyree had lost him in the 5 seconds he wasn't in view. However, the odd sounds drifting in front the ajar front door did draw his attention.

As he had anticipated, Kyree found Ambrose stood over a bruised and bleeding Tyrell. Kyree did not expect to two black horns parting Ambrose's dark locks, so that was why he didn't get angry. Obviously, he didn't want people to see them, Kyree didn't understand why, he thought they were beautiful, like the rest of Ambrose.

A tiny whimper drifted through the air as Ambrose's shoe came into contact with Tyrell's stomach. Tyrell clutched his leg, which was probably broken judging by the position it was in. He wouldn't be able to take much more. Kyree had to intervene before more blood was spilt on the property.

"Babe?" at the sound of Kyree's voice, the two horns disappeared and Ambrose glanced over his shoulder, his eyes that deep black Kyree loved.

"2 minutes, Ky, if that," Ambrose's voice was much rougher than usual, low and gruff, bearing striking similarities to an animal. Kyree leant against the stone wall, a silent debate raging in his mind for just a second.

"You know I can't do that, babe, as much as he deserves it. Come inside and let me help you calm down."

"I said 2 fucking minutes, Ky!" suddenly, Kyree was pinned against that same wall he had so casually leant against, Ambrose's hand around his throat. Oddly, he felt no fear, nor anger, just a strange sense of calm. And a heaping wave of arousal.

"Babe, you know I like it rough but out here isn't the best place. Don't want my mother or father seeing us now, do we?" Kyree stared into the endless black of Ambrose's eyes, a small smirk on his mouth. In an instant, the two men were in Kyree's bedroom. A succession of soft moans slipped from Kyree's mouth as Ambrose buried his face in his neck, nipping and sucking on the soft skin.

"Show me them again," Kyree whispered, dragging his fingers through Ambrose's dark locks. Ambrose bit down a little harder, sending a wave of pleasure rippling through Kyree, clearly trying to distract Kyree long enough for him to forget about what he had seen.

"Please, Amb," Kyree pleaded, forcing the demon to look him in the eye, "I wanna see them up close," Ambrose's eyes had remained black, yet they seemed to soften slightly when they connected with Kyree's hazel ones.

"Fine, just for a second," Ambrose caved, allowing the horns to grow. Kyree observed, a smile on his face. They were somehow a darker black than Kyree had ever seen a demon's eyes fade to, yet had a slight pearlish finish to them, almost shimmering in the light when Ambrose moved his head.

"Amb, they're beautiful. Why don't you have them out all the time?" Kyree marvelled, frowning a little when Ambrose stopped him from touching them, "are they sensitive?"

"Very," Ambrose murmured, releasing one of Kyree's hands from his grip, showing his trust in Kyree, "gently," he ordered. Kyree ran his fingers through Ambrose's hair before very gingerly touching the base of one of the horns. He heard Ambrose's breath hitch in his throat, his grip increasing on Kyree's wrist.

"Painful?" Kyree asked, ceasing his movements.

"No," Ambrose breathed, causing a smirk to curl Kyree's lips. He began to stroke his fingers around the base, inciting a groan from Ambrose.

"Feels good?" Kyree whispered, simply getting a slow nod in response as Ambrose succumbed to the pleasure consuming him. Keeping his movements gentle, listening to the soft moans from Ambrose, Kyree used his other hand to undo the buttons down Ambrose's shirt.

That was, until the door swung open, revealing a heavily tattooed yet rather petite looking man. Ambrose's horns dissipated to nothing, his dark eyes scowling at the man.

"Learn how to fucking knock, Deacon," Ambrose seethed, standing upright and buttoning his shirt again. Kyree frowned, a bemused expression on his face as he stared at Ambrose then the man called Deacon.

"Oh, Amb, you should know by now that I don't knock. It's much more fun to just walk in, you can't hide things from me then, dear," Kyree disliked the man instantly, his tone didn't match the smile on his face. There was something off about him, he made Kyree's instincts flare up.

"Who the fuck are you?" Kyree chimed in.

"Deacon Rome," the man stepped further into Kyree's bedroom, extending a hand for him to shake, "Ambrose's fiance," Kyree didn't know what to say, didn't even know whether to shake Deacon's hand or not. He hadn't thought previously about the fact that one day he was likely to come face to face with Ambrose's fiance.

"Why are you even here, Deac? No one invited, I specified that to Orion and Yennifer. You draw too much Goddamn attention," Ambrose grumbled, his eyes lightening to that mystifying grey-blue Kyree adored.

"It's called being polite, Amb, and keeping up fucking appearances. With you being AWOL, someone has to fucking act like you're not hiding. I came to wish your new boy toy happy fucking birthday," Deacon spat back. Kyree's frown deepened, Ambrose had said Deacon was a close friend, the way they were acting sure wasn't friendly.

"You came here to spite me, I'm not stupid. You knew I didn't want you here so obviously you had to come, just to fucking piss me off."

"You really think the fucking world revolves around you, don't you, Ambrose? Well, it doesn't. You aren't the centre of the damn universe, as much as you would love to be," Kyree's blood boiled as Deacon continued to address Ambrose in that manner.

"He's royalty, you can't fucking talk to him like that," Kyree chastised.

"Really?" Deacon scoffed, "I'll talk to him how I like. Don't you forget, honey, I'm the one engaged to him, you're just his boy toy. He'll get bored of you soon enough and throw you away like the trash you are," a small glint of silver caught both Deacon and Kyree's eyes as it hit Deacon's chest and fell to the carpet without a sound.

"Was engaged. Past tense," Ambrose corrected, "get out, Deacon. I'll have my father announce our split when I tell him about Kyree in a few days. I suggest you're moved out by then," Deacon's mouth hung open as Kyree ushered him from the room, closing and locking the door behind him. Ambrose was sat on the edge of the bed, his head hung in his hands. Kyree knelt in front of him but Ambrose refused to make eye contact.

"Hey, he's gone now, don't be mad."

"He's a fucking ass," Ambrose grumbled, "he had no reason to be here tonight, he just enjoys getting on my nerves," Kyree moved around to sit behind Ambrose on the bed.

"You're tense, relax, he's gone," Kyree began kneading the firm flesh of Ambrose's shoulders, coaxing a soft moan from his lover as his body started to unwind. Ambrose tipped his head back, his eyelids closed, giving Kyree access to that wonderful mouth of his. Kyree gripped the black lapels of Ambrose's expensive suit, tugging his demon closer to him, craving more of his touch. Ambrose groaned, giving Kyree full entry to his mouth, pulling the demon onto his lap so he was straddling him.

"I haven't got you a birthday present, baby," Ambrose muttered, grazing his teeth over Kyree's bottom lip.

"Mmm, you just broke off your engagement for me, that's a pretty good present," Kyree loosened the red tie around Ambrose's neck, reaching under to unbutton his shirt.

"Let me give you something more," Ambrose's hands wandered down to Kyree's belt, a glint of mischief flickering in his eyes. Kyree didn't reply, too busy leaving an array of purple marks across Ambrose's throat, revelling in the soft mewls of pleasure erupting from his lover.

Kyree's back hit the soft mattress under them and Ambrose took his time kissing down his firm chest as he opened Kyree's shirt. Kyree savoured the sight of Ambrose's head bobbing up and down as he pleasured his lover, an occasional glance upward to catch Kyree's eye simply adding to the enjoyment he was experiencing. Curling a fistful of Ambrose's dark locks around his fingers, Kyree lost himself in the intense feeling of his lover's mouth wrapped around his most sensitive area.

Ambrose was amazing, in every Goddamn aspect.

Chapter 12

"Fuck," Kyree hissed, lowering himself into the bath, the steaming water lapping against his aching skin, "this is not relaxing," he forced out through gritted teeth, glaring at Ambrose stood in the doorway adorning a small smirk.

"Give yourself a few seconds to adjust to it, Ky, it'll get better," Ambrose muttered through soft chuckling. Kyree's breath hitched in his throat as he submerged himself further in the water, the gentle ripples licking sullenly at the bullet wound still prominent in his chest and back.

"Would you like me to join you?" Ambrose queried when he saw Kyree looking no less tense. Kyree's curt nod was his only response. Ambrose stripped and slid into the bath behind Kyree, being careful not to touch the wounds he had caused. Kyree almost melted into Ambrose, savouring the feeling of his bare skin on the demon's.

"Better?" Ambrose breathed into Kyree's ear, catching the soft lobe between his teeth. Kyree simply allowed a soft moan to drift through the air as his eyes fluttered closed and his head lolled back against Ambrose's shoulder.

"So what now?" Kyree mumbled.

"What?"

"What happens now with Deacon? And your father? And us?" Ambrose trailed his fingers down Kyree's arm as he listened to him speak. He very much enjoyed the sound of Kyree's voice, it was smooth, felt as though it wrapped him in a silk blanket.

"Well, no doubt Deacon has already gone running to my father to get him on his side so I'll leave it for a few days. I'll tell my father how much I would dislike being married to Deac and he will probably send me grovelling back to him, tail between my legs, offering a much higher status than what it used to be. He will try to anyway, I'm not bending over backwards for that man anymore.""Only bending over for me then?" Kyree commented, loving the melodic sound of Ambrose's deep chuckle. Kyree had something else to say, something that most definitely wouldn't be making Ambrose chuckle. In fact, without explanation, it would make him do the complete opposite.

"What's on your mind, baby? I can practically see the cogs turning in your brain," Ambrose coaxed the thoughts from Kyree's mind, not realising how much he would dislike them.

"Maybe your engagement to Deacon isn't such a bad idea," Kyree said in a very soft voice, opening his eyes to glance up his frowning lover.

"What?" as expected, Ambrose didn't seem all that thrilled with the idea, "are you joking, Ky? You want me engaged to that ass? Is there something you're not telling me? Are you not invested in this-"

"You think I would wait to tell you that when we were in the bath together?" Kyree interrupted, "Amb, this has nothing to do with my feelings for you, which are there and definitely acknowledged, by the way."

"So what gave you this stupid idea then?

"I was thinking about something Idella said when he found out we had fucked. He said that if anyone found out the connection between us it would be a pretty easy ploy for exploitation. I mean, he was just talking about a one night stand, maybe our relationship out in the public wouldn't be the best idea," Ambrose inhaled deeply, lost in his own thoughts for a few seconds, leaving Kyree to rethink everything he had said for errors.

"So? If I married Deac someone would find a way to exploit that, whoever I marry people will use to get to me. It comes with the job. I would prefer it to be you that was exploited rather than Deac."

"If I'm your knight, I don't think I can be your husband. It's too risky. What if my feelings for you got in the way of something, or we had a fight and I wasn't around when you needed me to be?" Ambrose's stare softened, those grey-blue eyes filling with a little more emotion and a little less blatant anger.

"So don't be my knight," it was Kyree's turn then to frown, "Ky, if I have the choice between you being my knight, having to see you every day and not being able to express my affections, or you being my husband. I choose husband. Every time," Kyree remained silent, instilling worry in Ambrose, "unless you don't want to be my husband. I mean, I know how long people train to be knights of hell, I don't want to get in-" Ambrose had a tendency to ramble, Kyree enjoyed being able to shut him up with a kiss.

"If it was pick husband or knight, I would pick husband any day. I mean, with this dream thing we've got going and what Alexander said, clearly, our relationship is something more than normal."

"What did Alexander say?"

"You were there, Amb, did you just zone out after Alex called me bunny?" Kyree chuckled softly, breaking the wall of tension that had been building slowly between the two men, "he said we were destined for something important. I don't think we can do this important thing if we aren't together, so I guess, for the universe, I'll choose husband."

"Ambrose?" Yennifer's voice drifted in from the bedroom, rousing the demon from his daydream.

"In here," Ambrose uttered just loud enough for Yennifer to hear. She didn't look the slightest bit startled as her eyes landed on the two naked men, one of which being her own slumbering son.

"Your father is here to speak with you," how odd, Ambrose thought, his father never usually left their palace. Mostly for security reasons, but still, he wasn't expecting any sort of visit here.

"I'm a little incapacitated," Ambrose motioned to his sleeping lover laid over him, "tell him he can speak to me in here if it is so urgent," Yennifer left the bathroom with a small nod and in her place returned Ambrose's father. Lucifer Ross did not look his true age of nearly 3 millennia. Only his silvered hair gave away the fact that his body had aged to around 60, yet his skin was not creased and his face had no dullness to it.

"Father, to what do I owe the pleasure?" Ambrose smiled, feeling no embarrassment that his father could not only see him completely nude but also his lover.

"Deacon came to me earlier tonight," Lucifer leant against the counter opposite the bath, crossing his arms over his chest, "I did not believe his story at first, but now that I see you here, it seems very plausible," Lucifer's eyes flickered over Kyree's face, "this is him then? The Landon boy?"

"His name is Kyree, and whatever Deacon told you about him is probably untrue," Ambrose muttered.

"I thought you loved Deacon, Ambrose, I thought that was why you wanted to marry him. What do you even know about this Kyree? You've been around him for no more than 2 weeks, Deacon has known you for centuries. Why throw away your relationship for this man?"

"What relationship?" Lucifer remained silent, his head tilted to the left slightly as he awaited his son's elaboration, "father, I never loved Deacon. He's not even gay. There was no relationship between us, everything was simply platonic. I was with him to satisfy you, you're the one that said our pairing would be a good 'business deal' for hell," Lucifer looked bemused, his brows drawn together in a frown.

"But..." he began, his voice distant, "Ambrose, I told Deacon's father your marriage would benefit him too because I thought it was what you wanted. I pushed it so much so he would allow Deacon to marry you. I did it for you, I wanted you to marry for love, not for a business deal. I would never be so heartless," it was Ambrose's turn to adorn an expression of confusion.

"I never wanted to marry him, father, in fact, this engagement has torn our friendship apart. I only agreed to it because I thought you be disappointed if I didn't."

"Ambrose," Lucifer's expression softened, "your mother did always say our communication skills were awful, didn't she?" the two shared weak smiles, "if Kyree is the man you want to be with, and eventually marry, I support you," as if woken by the mention of his name, Kyree stirred, his eyes fluttering open.

"Mmm, evening, sleeping beauty," Ambrose murmured, pressing a kiss onto Kyree's hair as his father observed their interaction. The dazed smile on Kyree's lips drifted away as his eyes landed on Ambrose's father, his eyes widening.

"Oh my God," Kyree breathed, moving his hands down to cover himself, "Ambrose, your father is here, in the bathroom with us," Ambrose simply chuckled.

"I had noticed."

"Oh, wonderful. Did you just neglect to notice that we're both naked? This isn't really the usual 'meet the parents' setting, Amb," Kyree whispered furiously, his cheeks heating.

"I've seen many of Ambrose's lovers in compromising positions over the centuries, Kyree, it would startle me more if we met in a normal setting," Lucifer reassured.

"Well, since we are all conscious now. I actually have something else to confide in you, father," Ambrose interjected, "have you ever heard of two people sharing dreams?" Lucifer remained silent and averted his eyes to the ceiling, for Kyree's sake, as the two men got out of the bath and dressed.

"What do you mean by sharing dreams?" Lucifer queried in more depth as the three moved into Kyree's bedroom.

"I mean exactly that. I can see into Kyree's dreams as if I am a spectator in his mind. Like, just then, he was dreaming of walking along the coast hand in hand with me, throwing pebbles for Endwin to chase after," Kyree confirmed what Ambrose what saying with a simple nod.

"But I never get to see into your dreams, which is hardly fair," Kyree pouted in a teasing manner.

"Ambrose doesn't dream, never has, it used to drive his mother insane. She warned him that one day he would simply go mad because he wasn't able to work out his problems in his mind like everyone else. It is why, I believe, he is such a logical and literal thinker."

"You don't dream?" Kyree marvelled, his wide-eyed stare fixed on Ambrose, "you didn't tell me," Ambrose merely shrugged.

"I didn't think it was of any real importance."

"Maybe not to a normal person, but it could mean something because of this whole dream thing between us," Kyree turned his attention to Lucifer, looking a little sheepish as addressing his Lord, "do you know anything about it then, Your Majesty?"

"Please, call me Lucifer, you're practically family now. I don't know a thing, but I will search through your mother's possessions, Ambrose, she was always infatuated with phenomena such as this."

"Was?" Kyree attention returned back to Ambrose, who wore an irritated frown at the mention of his mother.

"My mother died a long time ago, and she was also infatuated with a hell of a lot of drugs. Whatever she thought up was probably from either an ecstasy or LSD induced hallucination. Most of what she uttered was complete shit, I'm surprised she didn't pass earlier," venom wove it's way easily into Ambrose's voice, startling Kyree just a slight.

"Amb, calm down," Kyree whispered, slipping his hand into Ambrose's in an attempt to reduce his lover's anger, "don't know why you offered to help me with my grief. You're clearly not the poster boy for dealing with your problems healthily," a small smile flickered across Ambrose's face, he knew Kyree was only teasing to try to snuff out the tension in the room.

"At least I'm not a sex addict," Ambrose retorted with a chuckle.

"Oh, you're missing out."

Chapter 13

2 extremely boring, uneventful weeks passed surprisingly fast. There had been no attacks on Kyree or Ambrose, clearly, the assassin was planning his next assault in detail. Neither Kyree nor Ambrose was looking forward to that.

"Baby, it's only a week, I'm gonna be fine and so are you," Ambrose cupped Kyree's pouting face, pressing a soft kiss to his lips.

"I still don't think it's a good idea. You're supposed to be in hiding and yet you're going to some big meeting thing with your father, the assassin will know you're there. He'll be expecting it," Kyree countered, "at least let me come with you."

"Ky, you can't, it will look too suspicious. No one is supposed to know about us yet, remember?" Kyree grumbled something under his breath that Ambrose couldn't quite make out, probably some choice curse words he didn't want to say directly to his lover.

"What am I supposed to do for a week without you?" Kyree changed the subject, accepting that Ambrose wouldn't change his mind even if Kyree promised him the world. He was as stubborn as a mule, actually, he was worse.

"Well, I was thinking you and Idella could take some friends up to the human world. Go camping or something, be humans for the week. It would be interesting for you, like a little experiment. And since my father will be with me and all the other dukes, I'll keep him off your back," Ambrose was grinning, but Kyree wasn't totally sold on the idea. He hadn't been up in the human world since he was shot, and before then had only spent a night at a time after Alexander's death.

"I seem to be a bad omen in the human world. Maybe taking other people with me isn't such a good idea."

"Kyree you are not a bad omen," Ambrose scolded in a much more serious tone, "you weren't shot because of any sort of karma or anything. And Alexander wasn't killed because of you either, you are not a bad omen. Don't say such stupid things, Ky," Kyree simpered, remaining quiet, "I have to go now, baby," Ambrose pulled Kyree into his arms, pressing a much more forceful kiss on his lips.

"You better call me or something, every night, Amb, I wanna know you're OK," Kyree demanded as Ambrose picked up the duffle bag he had packed.

"Every night, baby, I'll make sure of it. Have fun, don't spend too long missing me," with that, Ambrose dissipated into thin air, not giving Kyree a real chance to say goodbye. Kyree sighed, that awful empty feeling nagging at him the second Ambrose was out of sight.

"Idella!" Kyree called down the hall, waiting impatiently until his little brother's head popped out of his bedroom.

"Yes, brother?"

"Where are we going?" a grin grew across Idella's lips.

"It's a surprise."

"I hate surprises," Kyree grumbled, "is whoever is joining us also a surprise?" Idella simply nodded, "and when are we leaving?"

"Whenever you're ready, brother," Kyree took a deep breath, striding over to his brother.

"Whatever, let's just go now," Idella gripped Kyree's shoulder and, without a word, they were stood in a quaint little apartment. Kyree didn't recognise any features, although some items scattered around the room did seem vaguely familiar.

"An apartment? That's your big surprise?" Kyree was a little disappointed, Idella usually planned more interesting events.

"Kyree, God, you've gotten bigger," Kyree knew that voice. That deep, gruff voice that somehow dripped with warmth and happiness.

"Bishop?" Kyree spun on his heels, unable to contain the smile taking over his face as his eyes landed on the large man. Bishop was one of Kyree's oldest and dearest friends, yet he hadn't seen him for years. Well, Kyree hadn't really seen any of his friends since Alexander had died, he couldn't bear to see them happy when he was so miserable.

"No doubt you brought Rozelle with you," at the mention of her name, a petite black-haired woman stepped out from behind Bishop. She was tiny in comparison to her enormous demon husband, but Kyree knew not to underestimate the human.

"Kyree, you could have called, y'know?" Rozelle smiled her wicked little smile as Kyree kissed her hand, "always the gentleman, aren't you?" Bishop took it upon himself to engulf Kyree into a tight hug, a little startled when he actually returned it.

"That prince has got you all trained up then, has he?" Kyree shot a glare over to Idella, he had no right to tell Bishop and Rozelle about Kyree's relationship, "hey, Ambrose told us when he called us. He had to, it's not exactly a regular occurrence to get a house call from the prince of hell," Bishop explained before Kyree could start throwing punches.

"Who else is here? Just you two?" Kyree asked, a content smile on his lips as his anger dissipated faster than usual.

"Well, actually there is someone Roz and I would like you to meet," Bishop draped his arm over his wife's shoulders, a proud smile on his lips, "Pip, can you come here?" he called a little louder, keeping his eyes on Kyree. The door behind the couple creaked open slowly as a little-redheaded girl, looking no older than 5, stepped out sheepishly.

"Pip, meet your uncle Kyree," Rozelle said softly as the little girl stepped closer. Kyree bent down to eye level, his eyes flickering all over Pip's face. Her hair was long, stopping midway down her torso, laid in curls over her shoulders. Her eyes were a soulful blue, a little brighter than Ambrose's, Kyree thought.

"You had a child?" Kyree marvelled, not taking his gaze off the shy looking girl as she stood in front of him.

"Yes, a few years back. She's half demon," at the mention of her heritage, Pip's left eye darkened to a dazzling jet black, "half human. Pip, tell uncle Kyree your full name," Rozelle urged, although Kyree didn't understand the need to know the little girl's full name.

"Pip Alexandria Turner," Kyree's breath hitched in his throat, tears welling in his eyes at the little girl's whisper.

"You named her after Alex?" Kyree's voice was just as quiet as Pip's had been, "God, he'd be so happy," Bishop and Rozelle beamed at Kyree as he took hold of Pip's little hands.

"Hello, Pip. It's very nice to meet you," Kyree's tone was soft, not wanting to frighten the timid girl.

"Like from my bedtime story?" Pip questioned, her blue eyes wide.

"Bedtime story?" Kyree glanced up at Rozelle and Bishop, who both simpered when he made eye contact.

"The one with the knight and the prince, it's my favourite," Pip smiled nervously, chewing on her bottom lip.

"That sounds like a wonderful story, would you like me to make you something to eat and you can tell me it?" Pip nodded, lifting her arms, indicating she trusted Kyree enough to carry her. Kyree rose to his feet, swinging Pip into his arms, hearing a little giggle bubble from her as he carried her toward the kitchen. He sat her on the counter then set to work making her something to eat, listening intently to the story her parents had told her of him.

"Once upon a time, there was a knight called Kyree," Pip began, her voice growing as she became more comfortable in her surroundings, "and he was engaged to a man called Alexander. They were both demons and loved each other very much. One day, Alexander was taken from Kyree by some bad men," Kyree could feel the stares of Bishop, Rozelle and Idella, observing him to ensure he would not hurt the little girl, "Kyree was very sad for a very long time. He hid away from everyone because he was scared he would hurt other people. Then he met the prince, Ambrose, and he started to love again. Kyree let Ambrose into his heart right away, without even noticing how much he was changing for him. They were happy," Kyree placed a plate down next to Pip and she smiled, "that's as far as momma gets, she says the story isn't finished."

"Well, it sounds very interesting, no wonder it's your favourite," Kyree left Idella in charge of Pip as he returned to Rozelle and Bishop, his eyebrow cocked, "a bedtime story, Roz?"

"I wanted her to get used to you, she's nervous around new people."

"You wanted her to see me as the dragon slayer, not the dragon, I get it," Rozelle grimaced, assuming she had angered Kyree, "Roz, it's fine. I wouldn't want my kids around a man like me, or a man like who I used to be anyway. I'm better now, getting there, Ambrose is doing wonders. Just like in your story," Roz smiled, pulling Kyree into a hug.

"That prince really is taming you, isn't he?" Kyree chuckled, rubbing Rozelle's back.

"I think he might be the only one capable," Kyree wiped away a tear that had slipped past Rozelle's defences, "no crying, I'm sick of crying."

For the rest of that day, Kyree spent a lot of his time with Pip. She brought out something in Kyree, a part of himself that hadn't surfaced since long before he even knew Alexander. After a few hours observing the two, Rozelle and Bishop had relaxed, proving they did still have some trust in Kyree.

"So, Ky, you up for a little bar hopping tonight?" Idella queried over dinner.

"Why would I need to, little brother? I'm not single."

"You can go to a bar for reasons other than to pick up someone," Idella muttered, leaning back in his chair.

"If so, what will you be doing all night then?" Rozelle and Bishop laughed together quietly at Kyree's comment.

"Kyree, you're coming out with me tonight and that's final."

Chapter 14

Kyree had not missed bar hopping, not at all. The lights gave him a headache, the music was irritating, and the constant offers for sex were wearing away at his patience. He wondered how he had been so content in that setting for years yet he had been there only 20 minutes and already felt his sanity slipping away.

"Waiting on somebody?" Kyree glanced up from his beer, his eyes meeting that of a petite woman with lilac hair. Her skin was pale, paler than snow, the light hair framing her face making her look almost gaunt.

"Not at all," Kyree motioned toward the bar stool next to his, "sit, please," the woman did as was asked of her, ordering a cocktail that Kyree politely paid for.

"Trying to get me drunk?" she sipped her drink through a dainty straw, gazing up at Kyree through her half lidded, thick eyelashes.

"You ordered it, I simply paid for it. It is in no way my fault if you get drunk," the woman smiled faintly, examining Kyree with intent in her gaze.

"So, allow me to clarify. You're not waiting on anybody and you don't want to get me drunk so you're not here to meet anybody new. What are you here for?" persistent little thing, that woman. Kyree had hoped she would get the message and leave politely with her drink. He clearly overestimated her kind nature.

"My boyfriend is away for the week and my brother thought bringing me out would take my mind off of him," Kyree pointed at Idella sat at a booth with a dark skinned woman, "he clearly thinks shoving his tongue down her throat is attractive," the two watched as the dark skinned woman pulled away and slapped Idella, stalking out of the bar leaving him looking a little dazed. Kyree chuckled.

"That makes three, I should make a drinking game out of this, it would certainly take my mind off my boyfriend's absence," Kyree's attention returned to the woman, seeing she had not moved her gaze from him, "might I ask what you are doing here tonight?"

"I was searching for someone, as I have been for the past 6 months. And I think I may have just found him," the woman held up a piece of paper, her gaze flickering from it to Kyree over and over before a smile took over her face, "how ironic. I've been searching for this man for a little while and I find him here of all places. The precise bar he met my brother in almost 2 years ago," the smile faded slightly as the woman folded the piece of paper and stuffed it back into her purse, "do you remember, Kyree?" Kyree's brows drew together, his body immediately growing tense.

"Why are you searching for me? Because I had a one night stand with your brother?" Kyree felt the hostility welling within him, he wanted to leave, didn't want to lose control in the general public. It had felt so easy to calm down with Ambrose around him but now that he was alone his grip seemed to slip a hell of a lot faster.

"How about we go somewhere a little more private and I'll tell you everything you want to know?"

"Not gonna happen. Tell me why you've been looking for me and maybe I'll consider it," the woman sighed, standing from her seat and leaning in close to Kyree. To anyone else it would seem like some flirtation, even Idella wouldn't be suspicious, not that he was paying attention to his elder brother anyway.

"I know what you are, Kyree Landon," the woman whispered in his ear, "now, you're gonna walk out of here with me and we're gonna go have a nice chat. Like the sound of that, demon?" Kyree's blood ran cold, his body freezing up as the woman giggled and pressed a soft kiss to his cheek, furthering the act of their flirting to the people around them. In that moment, he had two options. Option One: kill the woman on the spot purely for assuming she knew anything about what Kyree was. Option Two, the more sane choice: leave with the woman, find out what she knew and what she wanted then kill her.

Silently, Kyree threw down a few bills to pay for the drinks then followed the woman out of the door. He didn't bother to inform Idella he was leaving, his little brother would be none the wiser of the woman that threatened their race's exposure after Kyree had taken care of the matter. It wasn't until the woman had foolishly led Kyree down a back alley that he spoke.

"This is private enough, tell me what you know," Kyree demanded, gripping the woman's wrist so she could walk no further. She spun on her heels, facing Kyree and, oddly, looking a lot less confident.

"You're a demon, that's about all I know."

"Demons don't exist, don't be absurd," the woman laughed softly, her eyes flickering around the alleyway.

"How are you stood in front of me then?" Kyree planned to roll his eyes and make another snide remark, though a swift strike to the back of his head prevented that. Whoever had hit him had put a considerable amount of force behind their swing, knocking Kyree forward onto his knees. He was hit again before he could make any sort of counter-attack, then a third time when his head made contact with the ground.

He could hear the woman screaming and two, maybe three, men yelling. The colours were swimming in front of his eyes, images shifting and turning. He had the urge to vomit, but the nausea passed relatively quickly. Obviously, the attackers thought he was human, assuming the three hits had killed or fatally injured him, and the continued sobbing of the woman proved the attack wasn't planned by her.

It took almost a full minute for Kyree's body to heal itself enough for the world to stand still in front of his view. There were three men, two holding down the woman and the third... Christ, what savages God's creations truly were.

"Fucking humans," Kyree seethed as he appeared behind the two men holding the woman down. Thankfully, the third froze in his heinous act when he noticed Kyree's eyes, void of colour. It was then that the sole of Kyree's shoe connected with his face, sending him tumbling away from the poor woman.

"What are-" the man on Kyree's left didn't get time to finish his sentence before Kyree alleviated him of his head. He didn't care about the blood spatter as he tore the jaw from the other man's head, leaving him to die a painful and slow death. It was the third he left the worst for.

"Your species disgusts me," Kyree growled, stalking over to the final man who was still struggling to pull up his pants, "if I had any say in the matter I would burn this world," Kyree kicked the man first in the stomach, then the chest, then the face, increasing in force with each movement, "no, actually, I would make your deaths much slower. I would enjoy watching dregs like you waste away to nothing," Kyree reached down and, to save you of the hideous imagery, ensured the man would not be able to procreate. Kyree allowed his demonic nature to enjoy watching the man weep and scream in pain as he bled to death.

"Are you OK?" Kyree asked as he wrapped his jacket around the woman, trying to preserve what little dignity she had in that moment.

"Y-Yeah, considering," the woman spoke in a shaky tone and Kyree realised his blunder, mentally kicking himself.

"Of course you're not, God, what a stupid question," Kyree scolded himself, scooping the woman into his arms gently, "do you live near?"

"Yeah, a few blocks from here," the woman was staring at Kyree, particularly his eyes.

"Alright, I admit it, I'm a demon. Now tell me your address."

"Is your brother here?" Kyree asked as he ran his fingertips over the top of some ornaments above the fireplace. He had heard the woman exit the shower and turned to see her stood in the doorway in shorts and a t-shirt, her long lilac hair dripping on the carpet.

"Um, no, he died about 6 months ago," she mumbled, wincing as she sat on the couch, crossing her legs. Kyree sighed, sitting opposite her.

"I'm sorry, again," the woman smiled weakly, averting her eyes to her lap, "you never told me your name. I would like something to address you by if I am going to explain half my heritage," her eyes flickered back up to catch Kyree's calm gaze, looking a little shocked.

"Saige. My name is Saige Harrison," Kyree nodded, sitting back on the couch to get a little more comfortable. It was going to be a long night.

"Why did you spend so long searching for me? If this was some conspiracy theory or little research project you could have just looked up demons online. For you to actively go out of your way to track me, it must be something more. Tell me," Saige bit her bottom lip, looking considerably more nervous at Kyree's request.

"Please, get to know me first. If I ask you now, you'll walk away and never look back. Give me a day, give me tonight, get to know me and I promise I will tell you after then," Kyree narrowed his eyes, debating the idea.

"OK, you have 24 hours, by this time tomorrow night you have to tell me, deal?" Saige nodded eagerly, then grimaced as she shifted slightly in her position, "off topic, are you OK? Do you need me to get you anything for the pain? Should I take you to a hospital? You're taking what happened tonight surprisingly well."

"I'm fine. I hurt a little but," Saige shrugged, a forcing a very weak smile, "it's a pretty common occurrence in this town with what I do," if Kyree had been in a cartoon, his face would have turned bright red and steam would be billowing from his ears.

"This has happened before?" Kyree tried very hard to keep his voice level, he didn't want to scare Saige, his rage wasn't directed at her.

"A couple times," Saige muttered and frowned at Kyree's bloodstained clothing, "don't you wanna shower and change? I have some of my brother's clothes that might fit you," Kyree knew she was trying to change the subject but it was too late. The beast inside him had been awoken, and it was hungry.

"Write a list," Kyree rose to his feet, unable to stay sat down as his fury built, "every person that has hurt you, write a list. In fact, every scumbag in this Goddamn town," Saige looked very startled, yet did as Kyree instructed. The list wasn't too long, under ten names so Kyree's trip would be less than an hour.

"He said you had compassion," Saige whispered as she held out the list, her hand trembling. Kyree took the list and clasped his hands over Saige's, bending down so he didn't tower over her.

"Saige, these people on this list, they are the dregs of humanity. I have compassion for those who deserve it, these people, they do not," Kyree pressed a gentle kiss on Saige's shaking hands, "I will return within the hour. Trust me, I will be in a much better mood to talk when I get back."

"Be safe?" Saige whispered as Kyree rose to his feet, making him smile just a little. Safety didn't matter to Kyree, he had to feed the beast before it started chewing away at his soul.

Chapter 15

It didn't surprise Kyree in the slightest that his first destination was a dark, dingy alleyway. Kyree had expected no more, the filth of the human world often hid in the shadows.

"Oi, mate!" a very northern English accent echoed through the alley, seeming to originate from in front of Kyree despite him not seeing any figures in his view, "you here to buy?" Kyree's still darkened eyes scanned the alley in front of him but he couldn't see a single soul.

"Yeah," there was a few seconds of silence before a door to Kyree's right swung open and three heavily tattooed men strode out. The middleman, though smaller than the other two, was obviously holding the authority in the situation, or so he thought.

"What you want and how much?" the middleman was trying not to look strain when looking up at Kyree, but was a good foot shorter than the demon. In the dim lighting, none of the men seemed to notice the blood soaking Kyree's dark clothes or the lack of colour in his eyes.

"Marcus White, Louis King and Craig Fisher?" Kyree inquired, glancing at the piece of paper once again before folding it and placing it back into his breast pocket. Simultaneously, the three men took a step back, a hand slipping behind each of them, obviously landing on a gun or knife in their back pockets.

"You a cop?" the middle man asked, hostility radiating from him. Kyree chuckled, stepping closer to the men, both to reduce the distance between them and to bathe himself in the artificial light streaming from an upstairs window.

"What the fuck..." the man on the left uttered under his breath, the others simply stood still and silent.

"I'm much worse than a cop. Your time on this world is over," a flash of silver caught Kyree's eye, the man on the left had chosen to die first. Kyree appeared behind him, placing a hand on either side of the man's head and squeezing. An awful squelching and cracking sound rang out as the man's skull was reduced to nothing but bone fragments and bloody flesh.

"Oh my-" the man who had previously been stood on the right didn't get a chance to finish his sentence before he turned and emptied the contents of his stomach onto the alley floor. Kyree took the opportunity to drag the blade he had acquired from the first man across the second man's neck, almost decapitating him with the force of his move.

"Get the fuck away from me!" the final man yelled, although his voice cracked and his hand shook as he pointed a gun at Kyree. Kyree's lips curled into a wicked smirk as he held out his arms, opening his chest up as a target.

"Take a shot, I dare you," Kyree taunted, taking slow steps toward that cowering man. Gunfire bounced around the alley as the man fired three shots, all missing Kyree, who, in a fraction of a second, had swapped his place with the man.

"How..." the man croaked out as he dropped to his knees, blood sullenly oozing from his wounds.

"Magic," Kyree said, disappearing into thin air.

The next two men were luckily meeting the only two women on the list down at some dock nearby. Kyree found that convenient, he would be less time than he had anticipated. Oddly, it was the two women that were harder to kill. Nevertheless, Kyree got the job done.

The final man was in a very different setting. Apparently, some big CEO of a fairly successful company, not the common criminal Kyree had assumed him to be. Had Kyree not been drenched in blood, he would have looked completely at home as he strode through the foyer to the front desk.

"Lander Maine, I'm here to speak with him," Kyree's tone was relaxed, yet the little woman sat behind the desk gaped up at him as if he just screamed bloody murder in her face.

"H-He's in a m-meeting," she squeaked, fear consuming her.

"I can wait, tell him not to be long, my patience has run dry tonight," Kyree said calmly before sitting down nearby, next to a very startled old woman, "Halloween costume," Kyree confirmed, flashing a soft smile to the woman next to him.

"It's June," the woman whispered, her body trembling as well.

"So I'm a little early," Kyree shrugged, fixing his eyes on a spot of paint flaking off the wall opposite him. It couldn't have been longer than 5 minutes until the woman told Kyree, in a very small voice, that he could enter Lander Maine's office.

"Good Lord!" Lander gasped in his gruff voice as Kyree entered the room, locking the door behind him.

"Lander Maine?" the man gave a short nod in response to Kyree, "wonderful," Kyree allowed the small knife he had hidden up his sleeve to drop down into his palm.

"What are you doing? You'll never get out of here, I have security swarming the building," Lander tried to bargain with his life, backing up against the wall as Kyree moved right in front of him.

"I have my ways," Kyree allowed the darkness to flood back into his eyes, making Lander's skin go pale as a sheet.

"I've done nothing wrong. On what grounds are you-"

"Lawyer talk won't work, Mr Maine. Does the name Saige Harrison ring a bell?" Lander grimaced, all the response Kyree needed, "you creatures are truly disgusting. You call us savage and impure yet it is you who truly deserves hellfire and the devil's wrath," Kyree drove the knife into Lander's torso, covering his mouth so the blood-curdling scream could not alert anyone to his actions. With very little effort, Kyree pushed the blade down through Lander's thick flesh, layers of fat and tendons cutting like butter with the demon's strength. It didn't take very long for Lander to cease struggling and the hand Kyree had clamped over his lips was of no use anymore.

Kyree's body had been mostly holding together the deep laceration down Lander's plump torso so when he stepped back he wasn't surprised to see Lander's insides spill out onto the floor. Lander's corpse landed in the pile of blood and entrails at his feet with a soft kind of 'splat' sound. It almost made Kyree laugh, but that truly would have been demonic.

"I truly am sorry," Kyree muttered as he collected the pieces of shattered glass up off the tiled floor, "I should have knocked or something. You obviously wouldn't be used to me appearing like that," Saige laugh lightly, holding out a bag for Kyree to put the glass in that she had so carelessly dropped when he materialised soaked in blood in her kitchen.

"It's fine, it's just a glass. No big deal. I wasn't expecting you to be so bloody, that's all," Kyree chuckled as he rose to his feet.

"Is that offer of a shower and clean clothes still on the table?" Saige tied the bag handles together and placed it on the counter.

"Of course," she led Kyree to the bathroom, taking a towel out of one of the cupboards, "my brother's old room is opposite, just pick anything from there that fits. He was a lot smaller than you," with a small smile, Saige exited the bathroom, closing the door gently behind her.

Kyree rested his head on the cool tiles lining the bathroom walls as the steaming water hit his tense shoulders. The events of the night had left him craving something, something he hadn't craved in a long while. He felt very alone, empty even, as he stood in the shower.

His body ached, his healing process still not working at full speed due to the bullet he took for Ambrose weeks ago. Simply thinking of Ambrose awoke Kyree's lust, at the rate he was going, he would have to turn the water much colder to surfice his comfort.

The irritating beeping of his phone roused Kyree from his thoughts. It was almost midnight, who the hell was calling him?

"Hello?" Kyree didn't care about the water on his phone, if it broke he would get another, although he did seem to remember reading something about it being water resistant.

"Well, I was expecting a nicer greeting, baby, but I guess that will do," Ambrose smooth voice drowned out all Kyree's anger with a warm, kinda fuzzy feeling he hadn't felt since Alexander was alive.

"Amb," Kyree breathed, closing his eyes as he rested his head back against the tiles once again.

"Are you in the shower? I can hear running water," Kyree allowed a lazy smile to take over his mouth, Ambrose did always notice the details Kyree wouldn't have even thought about.

"Yeah."

"At midnight?" Ambrose asked incredulously.

"I was unclean," Kyree said, chuckling.

"I might be able to spare a few minutes if you would like me to join you," Kyree could easily pick up the seduction in Ambrose's tone. He desperately wanted to say yes, physically aching and throbbing at the thought of it, but he didn't want Ambrose to know about Saige just yet.

"I'm just getting out actually, missed opportunity," Kyree turned off the water, stepping out of the shower.

"Damn, and I had such a boring day too. A shower with you would have been bliss," Kyree smiled, wrapping a towel around his waist with one hand, he could tell Ambrose was pouting, "anyway, I called so late because I only just got out of a stupid meeting regarding my fiance, or lack of one anyway. I debated outing our relationship just to shut up the old coots."

"Surely it can't be that big of a deal," Kyree lowered his voice as he left the bathroom and entered Saige's brother's room. Most things were packed into boxes with labels on them but there was still a lot out untouched. Kyree took one look at Saige's brother's sense of style and grimaced.

"You would think so, but they seem to think it would be a better idea for my father to remain reigning until I find someone else. Like I'm incapable of ruling by myself," during the time it took for Ambrose to formulate two sentences, Kyree had travelled back to his bedroom in Hell, picked out a pair of black sweatpants and a hoodie and returned to Saige's apartment, "baby? You there?"

"Yeah, yeah, I heard you. What's your father's opinion?" Kyree queried, realising just how difficult it was to put on a pair of sweatpants with one hand.

"He's on my side, thankfully, but that might just be because he knows about you. If they keep pushing this he'll either have to admit that I'm with you or agree with them."

"So tell them about us, would that truly be so bad? Why do they care so much about your relationships anyway, it won't affect them," Ambrose was quiet for a second and Kyree wondered if the phone had cut out.

"Um, Ky, it will affect them."

"How?"

"Ky, are you being serious right now?" Ambrose sounded baffled at Kyree's simple question, "whoever I'm with when I'm coronated will rule Hell with me," Kyree froze, every fibre in his body stopping simultaneously.

"What?" he managed to croak out, kicking himself for not thinking of this fact before.

"Ky, when I'm coronated, you will be too. You're gonna be a king."

Chapter 16

Kyree truly felt like an idiot. He had neglected to think far enough into the future to what would happen to his status when Ambrose was coronated. It was obvious, Kyree just hadn't bothered to acknowledge it.

"O-Of course," Kyree stammered, shaking himself from whatever paralytic state his mind had put him into, "can't believe something like that slipped my mind," Kyree added, forcing a distant chuckle.

"Look, Ky if- right now? Seriously? You can't give me five minutes?" Kyree listened as Ambrose fought with someone else, his voice muffled slightly as he held the phone away from his mouth, "fine, I'm fucking coming. Ky? Baby, I'm sorry, I have to go back. Meet me for lunch tomorrow? At that bar we met?" a small smile crawled it's way onto Kyree's lips as he remembered that first night.

"I'd like that."

"You'd better not be late. 12 o'clock on the dot, baby, love you," the phone cut out but Kyree didn't care. His mind was stuck on those last two little words Ambrose had uttered in a rush, two words that made his heart skip a beat and his head spin.

Kyree grasped the doorknob until his knuckles turned white, his breathing ragged and broken. No one had said those two words to Kyree since Alexander had died, everyone was too afraid. Maybe it was a slip of the tongue, yes, that must have been it. Ambrose wouldn't just blurt that out over the phone as some sort of parting gesture, it was a mistake, a simple little mistake.

"Sorry I took so long, Ambrose called..." Kyree trailed off as his eyes landed on Saige asleep on the couch peacefully, a small smile on her lips. Kyree tilted his head to the side a little, sharing in that smile, his gaze simply flittering over the slumbering human.

"Guess we'll talk in the morning then," Kyree muttered, scooping Saige up in his arms and carrying her to her bedroom. As he laid her on the bed, her grip on his arm tightened, confining him his position leaning over her.

"Stay with me?" she whispered, her fingers trembling just a little with the effort to keep herself awake and... of course, the fear of what had happened that night. She may have been able to put up a tough front but when her subconscious was let out to play, her guard was torn down easily. Kyree knew the feeling.

"Of course," Kyree scooted into the bed next to Saige, complying as she snuggled into his chest. Kyree had not experienced sleeping with a woman many times in his past, only a few when he was very young and still unaware of the intense attraction he had toward men. It was odd.

"You smell like death," Saige's soft voice drifted through the silent room, putting a smile back on Kyree's lips.

"I'm a demon, that's pretty natural," Kyree tucked a few stray strands of Saige's long lilac hair behind her ear, finally resting his hand on the small of her back.

"Tell me more, you promised," Kyree could hear the strain in her voice as she forced herself to remain conscious.

"Sleep, you need it, I'll tell you in the morning before I go see Ambrose," Kyree pressed a soft kiss to the top of Saige's head, tugging a little more of the covers over her.

"Who's Ambrose?" she murmured, allowing her eyelids to droop closed.

"My boyfriend."

"Tell me about him," Saige's voice was getting more and more distant as she faded into slumber, Kyree knew she wouldn't last long.

"Ambrose Ross," Kyree began, "he's gonna be the next king of Hell, and I guess I'm gonna be too. He's amazing, has such faith, such determination. Hunted by a faceless, nameless shadow yet still somehow sane enough to offer help to a man struggling with his own losses," Kyree paused as Saige shifted slightly, sighing happily with her head resting in the crook of Kyree's neck, "he's a little like you, in a sense. Somehow able to show such empathy yet never allowing anyone even a peek at his soul. Strong, so Goddamn strong. That man has enough strength for anything, a God would pale in comparison to him," Kyree sensed Saige was on the precipice of sleep and dropped his voice lower, "he's wonderful, Saige, you would love him. I don't know how anyone couldn't. I would give my life for that man, I would give anything for him," Kyree whispered, closing his own eyes, drifting into his own slumber. Or so he had thought...

Silence, the absence of noise, caused an innate fear to spike in anyone, so why did he not feel it? Whilst others cowered, whimpering and whining in the darkness, he stood still, listening to the movement of the air. Though, truly it could not have been silent, for the others around him could not just shut up.

"Ambrose," a voice whispered ferociously, "Ambrose, sweetheart, you need to come here," Ambrose knew the voice, yet ignored it.

"Amb, come here," his mother's voice remained at the same volume, it was her tone that changed. Ambrose detected fear, fear and desperation. The darkness formed thick walls around Ambrose, impenetrable by the naked eye. He felt lost, reaching out to find his mother, wanting to be held in her arms despite her insanities.

"Mommy?" Ambrose quavered, his frail body trembling as his hands clutched at the air in front of him. He had always hated the darkness, it was where the monsters roamed. His tiny feet shuffled across the concrete floor as he fumbled blindly for his mother. She would keep him safe.

"Ambrose, I'm here," he couldn't pinpoint her voice, panic swelling within the young boy, "follow my voice, I'm here," he couldn't. He couldn't follow her voice. It was growing distant, so he turned, but then it was silent again. Just the whimpering in the room. Who else was there? Who was with them? Where were they? Ambrose's mind couldn't keep up with the questions bombarding him.

"Mommy?" Ambrose squeaked, tears welling his eyes, "mommy, where are you?" the fear was growing insurmountable, consuming the young child. His tiny hand landed on something soft, the smooth warm fabric rising and falling in his grasp. He couldn't quite hold onto it like it was being tugged back every time his fingertips grazed over it.

"Momm-" a hand clamped over the young child's mouth, ceasing his speech as he was dragged backwards, away from the warmth. Ambrose squirmed and struggled but the vice-like grip kept him almost completely still. He was nowhere near the strength of the person, the thing, holding him.

As a final attempt at freedom, Ambrose sunk his teeth into the flesh of whatever was holding him, not letting up until even after he tasted the blood seeping into his mouth. It was bleeding, did that mean it was human? Or something else entirely?

"You're gonna stay very, very quiet for me, little boy," a gruff, male voice growled in his ear, sending an overwhelming tsunami of fear throughout the child, "or I will slaughter your brothers whilst you watch, got it?" Ambrose whimpered like a beaten dog, nodding his tiny head weakly. The man removed his hand, though Ambrose would have prefered it to have stayed there when he felt it brush over his taut stomach.

"Your innocence is..." the thing inhaled deeply, causing Ambrose to flinch at the sound, "intoxicating," the hand splayed out across Ambrose stomach, reaching out as if trying to touch all of his silky skin at once, "I'm going to take my time with you..." tears trickled down the child's face as a hand continued to caress his skin, the other gripped firmly around Ambrose's throat, barely allowing him to breathe.

Light. Blinding light caused the thing to let out an awful screeching noise before disappearing in a wisp of jet black smoke. Ambrose fell to his knees, sobbing uncontrollably, a melancholy wail that seemed to make the whole room shake as the child broke down.

"Amb? Amb, I'm here, you're OK," two frail arms wrapped tightly around Ambrose, pulling him into a tiny chest he knew all too well.

"K-Ky?" Ambrose whispered, his voice raspy with sobbing. Kyree shushed Ambrose, rocking him gently. The pitter patter of more small footsteps closed in, making Ambrose flinch and rear back.

"Amb, it's ok, it's just Fi and Dante. They made it light. They made it go away," Kyree rubbed Ambrose's shoulders, a worried smile on his little mouth. Ambrose looked up at the other two children, their hands clasped together, light radiating from their bodies, stealing Ambrose's attention as the shorter one spoke.

"Ambrose, mommy says it's time. We have to go..."

Chapter 17

K yree woke with a frown on his face, taking a few minutes to reassess what the hell he had just experienced. As well as this, he had to remember he wasn't laid with Ambrose, instead, it was Saige sprawled across his chest still asleep. Humans, all they did was sleep.

"You're late," Kyree's gaze flickered to the doorway of the bedroom, landing on Ambrose leaning there with his arms crossed over his chest, "and in bed with a woman, have something to tell me?" Kyree smiled, sliding Saige off of him gently and standing. With his finger on his lips, Kyree led Ambrose out of the room, closing the door behind him whilst they moved into the living room.

"That's only Saige," Kyree grimaced when he saw the time on the clock, 1:20, how had he even slept that long? Then again, he had done a lot the previous night, by which he meant he had gone on a small, controlled killing spree.

"Telling secrets to humans now, are we? I could have you prosecuted, y'know, I am a prince. I could do it myself even," mischief glinted in Ambrose's grey-blue eyes as he covered Kyree's mouth with his. Kyree moaned softly, giving Ambrose entrance into his mouth as he gripped fistfuls of his lover's hair. It had only been a night of separation but, to Kyree, it felt like a lifetime.

"I think we have more pressing matters to discuss," Kyree whispered, peeling himself reluctantly from Ambrose and sprawling across the couch, his back on the arm and his legs across the seat.

"Which are?" Ambrose's body fit perfectly into Kyree as he snuggled in between his legs, his back resting against Kyree's chest.

"The dream, Amb," Kyree massaged Ambrose's scalp, curling fistfuls of his hair around his hand whilst the other traced little circles over his lover's arm, "I think it was yours."

"I don't dream, Ky," Ambrose reminded Kyree, his brows drawn together in a frown as he stared across the room at nothing in particular.

"Yeah, but I don't dream like that. You were the centre, babe, not me. We were both children, and it felt so real. Like a memory, not a dream."

"That thing," Ambrose uttered softly, a shudder running down his spine at the memory of it, "it was awful. I could feel its power, when it touched me, it was like it was emanating it," Kyree buried his mouth in Ambrose's hair, pressing a few chaste kisses on his scalp in an attempt to calm him.

"Who were those other kids? Fi and Dante? And what was that thing with the light that they did? We were all no older than 5, how did they have that much power?"

"I don't know, Ky, but we gotta find out more about this dream thing. It's gotta be-" Ambrose stopped abruptly when Saige slumped out of her room, rubbing her eyes and yawning.

"Kyree, you didn't happen to-" Saige also paused when she saw Ambrose, looking startled, "oh, hello. You must be Ambrose, would you like some coffee?" Saige wandered into the kitchen area, completely at ease with the prince of Hell lounging on her couch.

"And you must be Saige," Ambrose appeared right in front of Saige, causing her to shriek and almost drop yet another glass, "what do you want with Kyree?" Ambrose towered over Saige, his eyes a soulless black, obviously meant to scare Saige into submission, or rather admission.

"Amb, don't frighten her," Kyree appeared next to Ambrose, slipping his hand into his lover's, "calm down, we have a deal," Ambrose didn't back down, simply leant in closer to Saige, awaiting her answer. Her eyes went wide as she shrank away, her gaze fixed on Ambrose's dark eyes.

"Ambrose Ross, stop scaring the poor girl," Kyree scolded, tugging on Ambrose's arm.

"I want him to turn me," Saige whispered, her voice shaking with fear. Kyree froze, his attention focusing on the only human in the room, the only person with a lack of respect for their own blissful mortality.

"You want me to what?" Kyree asked incredulously.

"Turn me," Saige repeated in a slightly more confident tone, despite her eyes never moving from Ambrose's, "please, I told you, Kyree make him stop, please," Kyree frowned, realising what Ambrose was doing, tapping into her fears like all royal blood demons were capable of. Kyree reached around, covering Ambrose's eyes, breaking the connection so Saige could stumble back, her body trembling.

"What a surprise, a human that wants to be a demon," Ambrose grumbled, gently pulling Kyree's hands from his eyes and brushing his lips over the knuckles, "let's leave, baby, I'll have Osiris deal with her," Ambrose said, his voice cold and emotionless. Kyree's attention hadn't wavered from Saige, as she averted her eyes to the tiled floor, somehow ashamed at her desires.

"Amb, we're not killing her," Saige's head shot up at Kyree's comment, hope in her emerald eyes, "I'm not agreeing to turn you, but I did promise to talk, so ask away. Anything you want, I'll answer truthfully," Ambrose didn't look too pleased but he also didn't interrupt again, instead busying himself with making coffee.

"Just tell me more about you. About demonkind. Everything, please," Saige perched on the counter opposite Kyree, watching him with intent and inquisitive eyes.

"Well, we're not as heartless as we're made out to be. We do have touches of compassion here and there. And we don't live in squalor, nor does Lucifer live out his days igniting us with hellfire. I would compare us to humans but that would be an insult, your race is much worse than us.

"Demonkind?" Kyree pondered, "well, we live under the rule of a royalty. Lucifer has been the only king I have ever lived under, but soon Ambrose will be coronated. We can materialise, which you have experienced first hand, and some of us-"

"Why do you want to be a demon?" Ambrose interjected finally, sick of listening to their casual conversation continue whilst that card was set out on the table.

"I'm alone," Saige murmured sheepishly, averting her eyes away from Ambrose's to avoid his hard stare, "I have no one in this world. I dropped out of school, I have no qualifications. I have nothing. My brother was the only thing keeping me alive, but he overdosed a few months back, I truly have nothing now. It was either this or kill myself. I thought I might as well try," Kyree knew then why Saige had wanted him to get to know her, she wanted him to sympathise. And he did. He had been through his own share of crippling losses, he didn't want her to live through hers in isolation.

"Do you know how you are turned?" Ambrose's tone was laced with venom, spite mixing in with it too, "Kyree marks you, then he has to kill you, then shares his blood with you. You will be eternally bonded with him however which way he wants you to be. That could be anything from lover to slave. You will be his, forever. Your freedom reduced to whatever mercy he is willing to provide. You will no longer be your own woman, you will be his pet," Ambrose seethed, and Kyree finally understood why his lover harboured so much rage toward the idea of Saige being turned.

"It would be paternal," Kyree reassured Ambrose, snaking his arms around his lover's waist, "I see her as a daughter so she would be my daughter. Nothing more, nothing less, babe. She would be your daughter too," Kyree rested his chin on Ambrose's shoulder, rubbing his demon's hips, "I would like to do this for her. But only if you give me your blessing," Ambrose was silent for what seemed like hours but was probably only a few seconds.

"Fine. It's not like we could have had a child naturally anyway. I guess this is the best we are going to get," Kyree pressed a chaste kiss to the corner of Ambrose's mouth before moving to stand between Saige's legs. He tipped her head up so she was looking him in the eye, those emerald eyes swirling with fear and anticipation.

"Are you sure you want this? It's permanent. Not something I can take back, no do-overs. This is forever, literally," Kyree said, not a glimmer of humour in his voice. He was deadly serious and Saige needed to know that. There was no going back once she agreed to this.

"I'm sure," Kyree patted her shoulder, a soft smile on his face, "never had a dad anyway, I imagine an eternity with two would be amazing," Kyree just about caught the twitch at the corner of Ambrose's mouth. He would warm up to her soon.

"The worst part is going to be the mark, OK?" Kyree took the dagger that had appeared in Ambrose's hands, it was ceremonial, only to be used when turning humans, "I have to carve my initials over your heart. They will remain there forever so if you can handle the pain, I will try not to make it too crude," Saige merely nodded, looking paler than usual as Kyree instructed her to remove her shirt, leaving her only in her black bra. When the tip of the blade first broke Saige's skin, and her warm red blood began to trickle down her chest into her lap, she made a soft whining noise, squeezing her eyes shut.

Kyree really did take his time carving his initials. When Saige finally opened her eyes and glanced down at her chest, Kyree removed the rag he had pressed over the bleeding wounds to allow her to see her new mark. 'KL' in cursive letters to the left of her chest, sullenly oozing blood yet somehow looking so beautiful.

"You still have time to back out, Saige," Kyree reminded her when a tear slipped from her eye.

"I'm finally gonna have parents, why the hell would I pass up that opportunity?" she whispered, a smile on her lips. That smile didn't even falter when Kyree slid the blade across her upper thigh, severing the femoral artery, giving her but five seconds to live.

In that five seconds, Kyree cut his own wrist and pressed it on the gash across Saige's thigh, allowing his blood to mingle in with what she was losing. Her body began to sway at the 3-second mark and Ambrose gripped her shoulders, ensuring she wouldn't fall into Kyree.

Saige didn't wake for a few days, as expected. Yet Kyree remained by her side the entire time, her hand clasped in his. Her body had to replenish her new blood, which would be almost exactly the same as Kyree's. He wondered if she would have the same intolerance to fire. He had been told he had hellfire in his veins, maybe that meant she would too.

"Kyree, we have a problem," Ambrose announced as he appeared in the room, looking exceptionally worried.

"Babe, if this is about the dukes not liking your lack of fiance, just tell them about us," Kyree responded, his attention focused on the unnerving absence of movement from Saige.

"Kyree, it's not about that. How old did Saige say she was?" Kyree thought back over the conversations he had had with Saige.

"She didn't say. But she was in a bar so I assumed she was no older than 20. She looks young so 19 maybe. Why?" Ambrose stalked closer, kneeling in front of Kyree, a worrying amount of fear in his eyes as he gripped Kyree's hands.

"She's 16, Kyree. You turned a child."

Chapter 18

Kyree was glad he was sat when his knees began to feel weak, his head starting to spin. The world rocked as his gaze somehow remained on Ambrose, that was until his lover became two men, then three.

"Kyree, breathe!" Ambrose's voice echoed around Kyree's head, desperation ringing in his ears. Kyree hadn't noticed it had been almost a minute since he had taken a breath, every fibre, organ and bone in his body paralysed with the realisation of his mistake.

As he inhaled forcefully, Kyree's chest heaved, his body silently scolding him for inhibiting such essentials. Ambrose's tight grip on Kyree's hands seemed to be the only thing keeping grounded, that and his new daughter laid next to him.

"She can't be," Kyree uttered softly, "her younger brother, he would be 20 now, she has to be older than that. A-And she was served in a bar, Amb, she was-" Kyree was babbling, clinging desperately to the fabrications that Saige had told him. He was drowning in fear, in regret, in emotion.

"She lied, Ky," Ambrose said bluntly, his gaze dropping to Kyree's knees, obviously unable to hold the eye contact with his fearful lover.

"What do I do, Amb?" Ambrose had not heard Kyree sound so vulnerable since he had first told him about Alexander, and what had followed that discussion was not a particularly happy memory for either of them.

"Kill her, no one would ever find out that way. You would be safe," Kyree's fear fizzled away as the tsunami of rage washed through his mind at the thought of harming Saige. She was his daughter now, and should have been Ambrose's too. Kyree wrenched his hands from Ambrose's grip, creating distance between them as he paced across the living room, trying to contain the paternal instinct to give Ambrose a black eye for suggesting he murder his own daughter.

"I can't kill her," Kyree seethed, refraining from making eye contact with Ambrose.

"Then we leave together and I'll get Osiris to deal with it. Kyree, please, you'll never see a body, he'll make it painless-" allowing the fury to take control for just a second, Kyree slammed Ambrose into the nearest wall, eliciting a soft groan and causing a moderately sized crack to begin a climb up said wall.

"No," Kyree growled, his face mere inches from Ambrose's and his hands clenched tightly around Ambrose's shirt collar, "you will not harm her," Ambrose remained irritatingly calm, resting his hands gently on Kyree's forearms, awaiting the dark cloud in his lover's mind to drift away.

"Baby, please, you don't deserve the punishment for this. She lied to you, please, let me fix this for you. Your bond isn't complete, she's not awake yet," Ambrose suddenly looked defeated, weary, frightened. Kyree loosened his grip, allowing Ambrose to rest his head on his shoulder and wrap his arms around Kyree's waist. Kyree glanced toward the couch and sighed, holding Ambrose against him in a tighter grip.

"Yes, she is," Kyree murmured, his eyes remaining on Saige's tear stained face.

"I'm sorry, Kyree," she whispered, her voice raspy due to her recent death, "I'm so so sorry. I didn't know, I swear to God I wouldn't have asked if I didn't know," tears began to flow from her emerald eyes once again, yet Kyree merely shook his head lightly, a lopsided smile on his lips.

"Don't apologize, it was my own fault. I should have been more careful, I should have asked your age. I just assumed-"

"Kill me, Kyree," Saige interrupted, her eyes wide with empathy for her new father, "Kyree, please, you have to kill me. You have to. This is my fault, you can't take the blame for this. Kill me, please," Saige begged, rising to her feet on wobbly legs, similar to a newborn deer. In a sense, she was a newborn animal, born anew as a demon.

"No one is killing you, Saige, this whole situation is my fault and I will take the blame for it. No doubt the dukes have sensed my mistake already and are sending someone to collect me," as if on some cue, two men in black suits appeared by the doorway to the Saige's room. Their gaze moved together, drifting from Saige's terrified expression to Ambrose's rage then finally landing on Kyree.

"Kyree Landon, you are requested before the council," one of them spoke, their black eyes set on Kyree in an intent yet emotionless stare.

"No, no, Kyree, you're not going. My father can make an exception," Ambrose stood his ground, tightening his grip around Kyree. Of course, that had no effect when Kyree simply appeared between the men, accepting his fate. He flashed what he thought was some sort of reassuring smile at Ambrose but barely felt his lips move so knew it was minimalist. Before the three disappeared, Kyree managed to ask Ambrose one final request.

"Take care of my daughter."

Kyree brushed his fingertips down the suit that had been laid out for him, no longer caring for the soft silky fabric as he once would have done. It was completely black, blacker than the night sky that illuminated the cell he was staying in. In the moonlight, Kyree could see a very faint silver inlay to the fabric, one that glimmered and glistened as he clothed himself.

The tie that had been paired with the suit was a stark white, contrasting so deeply with the darkness of the shirt and blazer that it almost seemed to glow. Kyree attempted a smile as he stared at his slightly less dishevelled reflection in the grimy mirror provided for him.

His eyes had lost that soft sparkle, the hazel iris' dull and lifeless. Deep purple bags sat under his eyes, standing out against his pale skin. He looked pasty, and he hated that. The worst part, he could feel his strength receding. His body felt a thousand times heavier every time he woke in that Goddamn place, he was weakening.

His appearance reminded him of some ridiculous human book, about a man making a monster. Frankenstein, they called the lunatic, Victor Frankenstein and his undead beast. As Frankenstein had once been, Kyree also felt he had become emaciated with confinement. Except, the monster he had created, the dead that he had brought back, was Kyree's beautiful daughter, and he could never regret the decision he had made. Even if it had unwittingly been his last.

The two men who had brought Kyree to that place appeared in the open doorway, obviously sensing Kyree was ready. They marched him down a long corridor, toward an ominously large dark oak door. In the seconds they waited as the door was heaved open, Kyree got the opportunity to appreciate the beauty of the oak carvings. He was about to die, appreciation of carpentry was all he had left.

The next room was much lighter, torches bolted to the wall providing most of said illumination. Lucifer did have a flair for the medieval era. There was no furnishing in the room, only the throne sat prominently in the middle. Kyree took a deep breath as he walked freely into the room, the two men following from behind rather than guiding him.

Lucifer was perched on the throne, looking regal as always, with two men either side of him. Yet all the power in the underworld and he still had such a grim expression. Lucifer had grown to care for Kyree, he was his son's lover. Acting out a punishment from the council upon that particular demon, one who had done nothing wrong other than turned a girl he believed he was helping, was a surprisingly difficult thing for Lucifer to comprehend.

As Kyree knelt in the middle of the room, his hands flat on his thighs in a sign of submission to his king. He allowed his gaze to drift. The room had not been silent, rather Kyree had just opted to drown out the sounds of crying with anything he could. The crackling of the fire on those torches, the sound of his footsteps, anything. Anything to prevent him from listening to his own mother's ragged sobs.

His mother was cradled in the arms of Kyree's father, who looked slightly more reserved yet still grief-stricken. A part of Kyree found that somewhat amusing, they were already grieving even though he was still alive. How odd. Idella was on the other side of Yennifer, his eyes bloodshot and puffy from previous tears despite none being shed in the presence of others.

A spike of pain jolted through Kyree as his wearied gaze landed on Ambrose and Saige, as though someone had pressed a white-hot poker over his heart, causing all of his suffering to resurface. It had been a month since he had seen either of them, a month since he had been put in that Goddamn cell to await his execution.

Both had been prohibited from visiting Kyree, although he was not entirely sure why. He didn't think he had any tears left in him, but felt the familiar sting of just one more as Ambrose tugged Saige into a hug, kissing the top of her lilac hair. Kyree knew Saige had begun to cry too, but Ambrose also knew she wouldn't want Kyree to see her like that, so encouraged her to sob into his chest instead.

Ambrose's eyes had too lost the light in them, almost entirely grey as he held his gaze with Kyree's. In fact, Ambrose had the same pale skin and dark bags under his eyes too. Kyree found it a little odd, yet allowed the thought to slip right out of his head. He had more important things to focus on.

"Kyree Landon," Lucifer began, bringing Kyree back to the here and now, drawing all attention to him, "you stand accused of violating our oldest and most sacred law, turning a child," Lucifer paused, whether it was to gather himself or for some sickening effect, Kyree didn't care. He had accepted his fate, had made peace within himself. He may not get to live out the life he wanted with Ambrose, but he had given him a child, the one thing Kyree did not expect to provide for a single lover. And with that, Kyree could pass in tranquillity, finally able to see Alexander once again.

"You have been found guilty of this charge, Kyree Landon, of which the only repercussion fitting is death," one of the men from before stood behind Kyree, swirling shadows around his hand. The shadows were hell's version of the lethal injection. Quick and painless. They even cleaned up after themselves, devouring any mess they made during the killing.

"Do you have any final words, Kyree Landon?" Kyree lifted his head, glancing over his shoulder to Ambrose. His lover was crying, silent, but still crying, tears streaking down his cheeks.

"Ambrose?" Kyree uttered his lover's name for the penultimate time, allowing his mouth to curve up ever so slightly as the memories of their time together flickered across his mind. Their first night together, when their lives seemed so much more normal yet so much more boring. Their time on earth, with Endwin in the park, their little moment of domestic humanity up there in the simplicity of it all. Just every moment in one another's presence, mere intense, unimaginable bliss.

"Ambrose Ross, I love you too," time seemed to stand still as Kyree watched Ambrose register the words that he had spoken. Ambrose's lips parted, his eyes growing more watery as the two men stared at each other, longing to embrace one last time.

Abruptly, the moment between them was shot down as a pain so unbearable, so overwhelming, pulsed through Kyree's head that it forced some sort of strangled groan from his lips. Covering his eyes, plunging himself into darkness in an attempt to relieve some pain, Kyree cradled his head, a long drawn out howl of suffering slipping from his lips. He had never felt such agony.

It was like a burning throb behind his eyes, each wave making Kyree feel as though his skull was being splintered open. He wanted to pass out, his mind screaming for his body to slip into some unconscious state, unable to stand the sensation.

Then, as quickly as it had started, the ache faded.

Kyree removed his hands from his face, his eyelids flickering open. Gasps erupted through the room as everyone stared at Kyree, all but Lucifer. Kyree followed Lucifer's gaze, his eyes landing on Ambrose crouched on the floor holding his head with Saige next to him, looking particularly worried.

"Kyree, your eyes..." Ambrose whispered as the two made eye contact, both simultaneously taken aback. Kyree did not know what had happened to his own eyes, but he assumed it was the same as Ambrose's. His lover no longer had two grey-blue eyes. He had one.

One grey-blue iris and one hazel.

Chapter 19

"What is this?" one of the men on the left of Lucifer bellowed, "execute him!" Kyree didn't have the time to protest before the man still towering over him touched the shadows to his cheek. They were strangely cold as if ice had been pressed lightly against his skin.

For a second, Kyree heard raised voices, desperation and anger filling the room. Then nothing. Pure silence and complete darkness. Even the fire seemed to cease it's sullen crackling, awaiting the verdict on Kyree's life.

"Retract the shadows," Lucifer's voice sounded muffled and distant, yet Kyree could still detect the grim tone he held. The darkness receded, warmth flooding Kyree's shivering form as he blinked rapidly.

"That's not possible..." the same man breathed, his wide-eyed gaze fixed on Kyree. Ambrose, who had previously been crouched on the floor a few feet from where Kyree was knelt, appeared just inches from his lover, reaching out to touch his cheek.

"I thought I'd lost you," Ambrose whispered, his voice barely audible despite how close he was to Kyree. Ambrose caressed Kyree's cheek, the skin on skin contact sending a flush of heat through the demon's freezing body.

"You can't get rid of me that easily," Kyree replied, leaning in and covering Ambrose's mouth with his own. He had missed his lover, craved his touch every day they had been separated. Allowing himself to relax for the first time in 30 days, Kyree sighed happily against Ambrose's soft lips.

Ambrose pulled away abruptly, inhaling sharply and tugging his sleeve up. The two men observed as a brand in the shape of chain weaved it's way up Ambrose's forearm, searing the flesh as it went. Kyree pulled up his own sleeve, seeing an identical mark growing on his own arm.

"I can't feel it," Kyree murmured, running his thumb up the freshly burnt skin of his arm, "must be my intolerance to fire."

"This is ridiculous!" that same irritating duke shrieked, stepping down from his position next to Lucifer and stalking over to Kyree and Ambrose, "this must all be some well thought out ploy, my Lord, your son is clearly just stalling the execution for his own purposes. I suggest-"

"Silence yourself, Idris!" Lucifer bellowed, his voice echoing in the bare room, "you have spoken enough, should another word leave your mouth I will remove your tongue. You are lucky that Kyree somehow survived your attempt on his life or your tongue would not have been the only appendage I would have alleviated from you," Lucifer appeared next to his son, helping both him and Kyree to their feet, "may I see?" Kyree presented his arm to Lucifer, who examined it with extreme care, his brows drawn together in a frown, "there is clearly a higher power at work here, Kyree Landon, you are pardoned of all charges. I have no right to enact any sort of punishment upon you with your growing tie to my son, you have my deepest apologies."

"It's fine, you were only doing your job. I forgive you," Lucifer left with the other dukes and Kyree's family, leaving the demon alone with Saige and Ambrose.

Kyree, with one arm on the waist of Ambrose, turned to look at his daughter. She looked less frail, her body filled out slightly more with toned muscles. Her hair had grown somewhat and the mark Kyree had given her over her heart was framed with black and red flowers that had been tattooed onto her pale skin. Kyree held out a hand to his daughter, a broad smile on his lips for the first time in what felt like forever.

"Come here," Kyree encouraged, cradling his daughter as she wrapped her arms tight around his neck, "you have flourished, my dear," Kyree murmured against her hair, his grin widening when he noticed Ambrose also had a hand on Saige's back.

"I missed you so much," she breathed, looking up at Kyree with tear-stained cheeks.

"I missed you too, my dear, I wish I could have been with you in your first few days. Although, it does seem Ambrose has taken good care of you," Kyree glanced at his lover, pressing a chaste kiss to his lips, "thank you."

"It was practically your death wish, baby, I wasn't going to ignore it. Besides, you did say she was my daughter too, I wouldn't abandon her," Kyree felt a warmth in his heart he hadn't experienced for so long. The warmth of love, of desire and of true complete happiness. He was reunited with his family, his lover and his daughter. What more could he want?

"A shower," Kyree declared as he entered his bedroom in the Landon mansion, Ambrose following on his heel, "I am going to take a nice, long, hot shower and you, Ambrose Ross, are going to join me," Kyree draped his blazer over the back of the chair by his desk, turning to face Ambrose. Kyree reached out to unbutton Ambrose's shirt but his lover shied away, causing a frown to sit rightfully upon Kyree's face.

"Ambrose?" Kyree uttered gently, but Ambrose turned away, his eyes averted to the floor, "babe? Did something happen whilst I was gone?"

apprehension swelled within Kyree, he had been gone a long time, maybe Ambrose no longer had the same feelings as before.

"I'm just tired," Ambrose muttered, obviously trying to hide the shakiness in his voice, "nothing is wrong. Go for your shower, I'm just gonna go straight to bed. It's been a long day," Ambrose started toward the door but Kyree gripped his wrist, preventing him from leaving.

"Ambrose, please, tell me what's wrong. Is it something I did? Did you meet someone whilst I was-"

"No," Ambrose interjected, his tone adamant and forceful, "no. You did nothing wrong, Kyree," Kyree tugged gently on Ambrose's wrist, encouraging him to face the demon. When he finally did, Kyree saw dismay plastered across Ambrose's soft features.

"Amb, what is it?" Kyree asked softly, tipping Ambrose's head so he was forced to make eye contact.

"The assassin," Ambrose whispered, his bottom lip catching between his teeth, "from the second you left, he started his attempts again. That's why we couldn't come to see you, I didn't want to lead him there."

"Ambrose, you weren't scared of him before, what changed?" Ambrose took a long, shaky breath before continuing, only adding to the fear building within Kyree. Ambrose hadn't even looked so vulnerable at Kyree's execution, whatever had happened had really gotten to him.

"He's becoming bolder. No longer content with the long-range shot, he's brazen. He attacked Saige and I when we were training, that was the last time he used a gun. We were both fine, I got shot in the shoulder but I promise you I tried my best to ensure Saige never got involved.

"But then, just a few days later, even after I had upped my security, he made another attempt. I was in here, Osiris was in the hallway and Anubis was below the window. I felt safe. I always feel safe in here, made me feel like you were still with me. But..." Ambrose paused, composing himself before more tears began to fall, "he caught me off guard, tried to garotte me with some piece of wire," Ambrose unbuttoned his collar, pulling the fabric away from his neck.

Kyree gasped, his eyes landing on the deep purple bruising surrounding a thin, half-healed cut wrapped around Ambrose's throat. His grazed his fingertips over it ever so gently, his jaw clenched at the thought of the coward that had done something so awful to his lover.

"Osiris got to me just in time, but he got away. It had been dim in the room, and he was wearing a hood. Anubis didn't even see where he went when he left through the balcony. But, it gets worse. He got into the water tank somehow," Ambrose began to unbutton his shirt, his eyes still on Kyree's, who was sharing in the pain expression, "I was taking a shower, and he put acid in the water mains," the shirt slid off Ambrose's shoulders and drifted to the floor as he cautiously turned away, presenting his back to Kyree.

Kyree had to cover his mouth to refrain from making any sort of sound at the sight of Ambrose's back. The previously smooth, tan skin was now a mangled, reddened mess. Kyree ran his fingers gently over the wounds, tears clouding his vision around the edges.

"It's healing, but it will scar. I didn't want to show you because I know how ugly it is. I understand if you're repulsed," Ambrose whispered, his head hung in shame. Kyree remained silent for a few seconds, trying to fully take in what had happened to Ambrose whilst he had been gone.

Kyree knew appearance wasn't everything to either of them, but he understood that Ambrose would be self-conscious of his scars, hell, Kyree would be too if it were him. Closing the distance between the two men, Kyree pressed his chest against Ambrose's back, eliciting a sharp gasp from his demon as he brushed his lips over his neck.

"It is not ugly," Kyree whispered between each kiss, planting the last one on the spot just above the top of the scar, "it is a part of you therefore it is beautiful," Kyree trailed a line of soft kisses along the highest ridge of the scar, listening to the succession of quiet moans slip from Ambrose as his breathing grew just a little more erratic.

Ambrose spun on his heel, pulling Kyree's head toward his, their lips crashing together. As Kyree backed Ambrose up to the bed, their lips desperately grabbing at one another, clothes were shed from them both. Kyree's shirt whispered to the floor after a short period of Ambrose fumbling with the buttons then finally just tearing the remaining ones from their place, scattering them across the floor.

Kyree pushed Ambrose's chest gently, encouraging him back onto the bed, loving the attention he was showered with as he removed his belt and stripped down slowly to his dark grey boxers. Ambrose's eyes wandered over Kyree's form, mapping out his body silently as though it may have somehow changed since they were last together.

"You're just teasing now," Ambrose muttered, his voice husky with lust and dripping with seduction. Kyree chuckled softly as he continued picking up the rest of the clothing strewn across the room, folding it before placing it upon the chair where he had laid his jacket earlier.

There was a smirk on Ambrose's lips as Kyree returned to the bed, straddling his lover's lap. Ambrose glanced up at Kyree through half-lidded eyes, his long dark eyelashes blending in with the jet black that had seeped into his eyes. Kyree peppered feather-like kisses across Ambrose's shoulder, sucking dark bruises into his prominent collarbone, deciding he very much liked the colour of deep purple on Ambrose.

Kyree wasn't all that interested in the sex they had that night, not to say that he didn't enjoy every minute with Ambrose, but it was the intimacy that he had truly savoured. It was as though every touch, every kiss, set Kyree's body alight with the love he shared for Ambrose.

He had craved Ambrose in the weeks they had been parted, not only craved his body but craved his emotions. His empathy, his happiness, everything. Kyree could sense every emotion that crossed through Ambrose's head and being separated, feeling his grief and anger without being able to help with it, it very nearly broke him.

As they laid together, tangled in a mess of sheets and limbs, hands clasped together, Kyree smiled a sated smile. Ambrose was sound asleep, no dreaming, as usual, just a peaceful blankness occupying his unconscious thoughts. As cliche as it sounded, Kyree enjoyed watching Ambrose sleeping. Smiled when his nose twitched, moved closer when that little frown formed on his face, whispered things he had yet to muster the courage to say to him during their waking hours.

It was as Kyree was muttering something under his breath that he felt the bed dip down to the left of him. Glancing over his shoulder, he saw Saige curled up next to him, her emerald eyes filled with a worried fatigue.

"I couldn't sleep," she whispered, "Ambrose let me sleep with him when I had nightmares. I didn't think you'd be awake, do you want me to leave?" luckily, Ambrose had mentioned something about waking up with Saige in his arms more nights than not, so Kyree had ensured they both put on sweatpants before sleeping. Just in case.

"Come here," Kyree ended up laid on his back, with Ambrose curled up on his right and Saige in the exact same position on his left, their heads both reclined on either side of his chest, Kyree's arms around both of their waists. He observed the both of them for a few seconds before finally succumbing to his own exhaustion, a smile on his lips and a warmth in his heart at his family being reunited.

Chapter 20

The water rippled in a delicate manner, licking sullenly at Kyree's fingertips as he dipped them into the pond. He wanted to touch the fish, wanted to know what their scales felt like under his skin. For weeks, he had been trying to catch one, the big blue one with the long white fins. Yet it always somehow eluded him, no matter how much food he offered and no matter how slow his movements were.

As the frail white fin slipped through the young boy's outstretched fingers, he gasped, his little eyes lighting up with hope that today it might just still long enough for him to stroke his fingers over the cobalt scales. Wiggling his fingers in the cool water, Kyree encouraged the small animal closer, holding his breath as it neared him.

Then it happened. The fish brushed up against Kyree's fingers as it swam past and he finally knew what the tiny animal felt like. The scales were smooth and almost glossy as they skimmed against the pads of Kyree's fingertips, sending a flush of cold throughout the young child.

He giggled triumphantly, lifting his hand from the water, watching the fish duck down into the darkness of the bottomless pond. For just a second, the thought of joining the fish in the pond flitted through the child's mind. To dive deep into the clear waters, venture into a world unknown to him, it was somewhat tempting.

"Daddy, where do the-" Kyree ceased abruptly as he turned, coming face to face, or rather face to chest, with a very tall man. A very tall man with a very sinister look in his eyes, a twisted smirk on his lips and what looked to be blood on his shirt.

"What were you saying, little boy?" Kyree had an awful fuzzy feeling in his stomach that whatever was stood before him was not a man. Rather, it was a thing. A thing that spoke in sort of a husky growl, almost hissing out certain sounds, as though it was a mixture between a snake and a bear.

"W-Who are y-you?" Kyree stammered, a wave of fear washing over the child, "w-where's my daddy?" the creature loomed over Kyree, it's emotionless eyes narrowed as it stared, unblinking, at the young boy.

"I asked you a question, little boy, so..." the creature leant down, so close to Kyree's face that he could feel it's heated breath on his cheek, "answer me!" it shrieked, startling Kyree so much that tears slipped from his eyes.

"I wanted to know where the fish went when they swam away," Kyree quavered, his body trembling as he stared into the colourless eyes of the thing.

"Well, how about I show you?" Kyree cried out as he was swung into the air and plunged into the deep waters of the pond. He thrashed his arms and legs as his head was held under the water, panic spiking his instincts.

But the little boy only had so much fight in him, with the sudden flush of ice cold throwing his body into shock and knocking all air from his lungs. It was mere seconds before the thing no longer had to hold him under the water. He didn't have the strength to lift his head out.

The burning sensation in his chest felt like a fire was growing in his lungs, searing into his flesh and extinguishing the life within him. Through half-lidded eyes, he could see the low sunlight streaming through into his watery prison, fluttering left to right as if it were waving off to him as he passed into unconsciousness.

It seemed surreal but the reality was pain to the child. Agonising pressure spreading throughout his frail figure as it screamed at him for oxygen, begging and pleading with each slow heartbeat. Somehow, Kyree knew that if he breathed in the water, allowed the cold liquid into his chest, that he would go faster.

He just had to fight the instinct to close his throat off, had to muster the strength to die that he could not grasp to live. Just one breath, one breath and his suffering would end.

Just...

One...

Breath...

A small hand gripped one of Kyree's arms, then the other, tugging his body roughly from the water. Another pair of hands aided in the struggle of pulling Kyree from the pond. Kyree coughed and spluttered, gasping for air the second he felt the breeze on his cheeks.

"Ky? Kyree, you're OK now, you're safe," a hand splayed across Kyree's back, spreading warmth through his body as he wheezed, his entire body shivering.

"What happened to daddy? What was that, Fi?" Kyree whimpered, staring up with a terrified expression at the two boys that had quite literally saved his life.

"We don't know, Ky. One of them attacked us before we came out here, we can't find anyone else," at the mention of the other members of their family, Kyree felt a spike of terror jolt through his chest.

"Ambrose," he uttered softly, stumbling to his feet and running inside as fast as he possibly could. Ambrose was in the basement, he had to get to him. Just as he reached the door, a hand on his shoulder stopped him dead in his tracks.

"Let us go first, Ky, light scares them away," Dante whispered, slipping his hand into Fionn's before turning the doorknob. Kyree shielded his eyes from the blinding light emanating from the two other children, only forcing them open when he heard Ambrose's sobs. Kyree darted blindly into the room, regaining a small amount of his vision as Dante and Fionn dimmed their light.

"Amb? Amb, I'm here, you're OK," Kyree reassured the child as he flung his arms tightly around him, tugging him into his little chest, hoping his erratic heartbeat wouldn't be too detectable.

"K-Ky?" Ambrose's voice was raspy and broken as Kyree shushed him, rocking the young boy gently in his arms. Ambrose suddenly tensed, rearing back as Fionn and Dante entered the room.

"Amb, it's OK, it's just Fi and Dante. They made it light. They made it go away," Kyree rubbed small circles into Ambrose's trembling shoulders, forcing some sort of smile on his mouth in an attempt to convey some calm aura. Ambrose seemed mesmerised by the light from Fionn and Dante, as if he had never seen their power before.

"Ambrose," Fionn spoke softly, not wanting to scare his little brother any more than he already was, "mommy says its time. We have to go..."

Awakening didn't come easily to Kyree. He woke with a cry, his eyes widened in terror and his heart beating so fast he feared it might leap from his chest. Ambrose was at his side in an instant, his tight grip on Kyree's arms being the only thing keeping his lover grounded in that moment.

"Ky? Kyree, calm down," Ambrose said firmly as Kyree struggled with controlling his erratic breathing, "Kyree, it was a dream, OK? You're safe, Kyree, you're safe," Ambrose kept repeating that as if he was not only trying to convince Kyree of that but also himself. It took time but Kyree relaxed soon enough, his breathing slowing enough to be classed as regular, rather than hyperventilating.

"That was awful," Kyree uttered between deep, laboured breaths, "so fucking awful, Amb. I felt it, I felt myself drowning. The breathlessness, the panic, the ache. All of it," tears welled in Kyree's eyes as he held into Ambrose's hands so tight his knuckles turned white, "what does it mean, Amb? Why the fuck are we haunted with these dreams? First yours, now mine. Is Saige gonna get one too? What is it?" Ambrose rested his head against Kyree's, caressing his cheek gently.

"I don't know, baby, I really don't know," Ambrose muttered, sounding defeated and weary. Kyree wrapped his arms around Ambrose's waist, leaning back and tugging him onto his chest.

"There's something deeper going on with us," Kyree murmured into the silence of the room, running his index finger down the spiralling chain brand on Ambrose's left forearm, staring into his lover's beautifully different eyes.

"Maybe I should get my father to ask around, see if anyone has seen anything like this before," Ambrose suggested, sliding his palm up against Kyree's, a smile tugging at the corners of his mouth when Kyree's fingers interlocked with his.

A sudden surge of power through the two men left them frowning at their hands clasped together. What began as a soft, barely visible amber glow, seeped down the two men's arms, igniting the blood in their veins.

"Ky, what is-" then two became one. There was no longer Kyree and Ambrose sat together on the bed in each other's arms. One being had taken their place. A concoction of the two men, incorporating the both of them into one body.

Rising to it's feet, the being strode on wobbling legs toward the mirror to look at itself. It had to lean over to see it's face, being well over 7 foot in stature and built like an ox. Broad shoulders, rippling muscles covered in taught tanned skin, glowing amber veins pulsating through the being. The sight was mesmerising, to say the least.

Short, brunette locks fell messily over the being's face, parted by the two thick black horns sprouting from it's head. They were longer than Ambrose's, curled at the tip, still that beautiful pearlescent shade of obsidian. The colour that matched the eyes of the being, staring intently at itself, wondering what on earth had happened.

The creature had strong features, a mixture of Kyree's perfect jawline and high cheekbones and Ambrose's full lips and somehow soft, compassionate eyes. The brand was still there, glowing a somewhat bright black, almost looking as though it was giving off wisps of charred smoke.

"Amb? Ky? You awake?" the being's gaze whipped to the door as Saige entered, her jaw dropping open when her eyes landed on the being. It saw her take in a breath to scream but knew it's reflexes were much faster than hers. In some miniscule measurement of time smaller than a second, the being clamped it's hand over Saige's mouth, kicking the door shut so no one would see their encounter.

"Do not scream," the voice that escaped the creature's mouth was neither that of Kyree or Ambrose. It sounded distorted, low and wild. The desperation only added to the gruff and husky tone. Saige's eyes were wide, yet she remained completely still as she stared at the being looming over her.

"Saige, do not be afraid. I am Ambrose. And I am Kyree."

Chapter 21

Saige, terror dulling her glistening emerald eyes, merely stared up at the creature, her petite body trembling. She was surveying it, her pupils dilating and constricting as they flittered over it's face, searching for something to grasp onto, something to trust.

"Are you calm?" the creature asked, it's own darkened eyes latched onto Saige's, "do you trust me?" Saige nodded weakly, seeming strong despite the tear trickling down her pale cheek. Cautiously, the creature removed it's enormous hand from Saige's mouth, pity beating in it's heart when she let out a soft whimper.

"H-How?" she whispered incredulously, "i-is this a normal demon thing? Is this gonna happen to me?" the creature backed up slowly, assuming Saige would want some distance yet she followed, reaching out to run the backs of her knuckles down the skin of the creature.

"No, this is definitely not normal," the creature murmured, trying to focus on Saige's face rather than her freezing hand trailing ice down it's cheek. She gasped softly as two lines of frost followed the track of her fingers, turning the amber veins a deep blue.

"What are you?" she breathed, the soft pads of her fingertips continuing their path down the creature's neck and over it's collarbone. The creature sucked in a laboured breath, a shudder running through it as her fingers neared the brand. The second her skin made contact with the blackened mark, the deep amber glow returned, growing to a blinding peak.

When the light finally dimmed, the creature was gone and in it's placed was Kyree and Ambrose, hands still clasped together. Stunned, the two demon men and their daughter merely stared at one another, wondering who would be the first to muster up some form of communication.

"That was..." Ambrose began, stroking his fingers up the brand, feeling the subtle burning sear through his flesh.

"Amazing," Kyree finished his lover's sentence, a broad grin on his lips, "Amb, that was fucking amazing. Tell me you felt it, felt the power surging through that thing. It was exhilarating," Ambrose chuckled softly at Kyree's excitement, snaking an arm around his demon's waist and pressing a chaste kiss to his lips.

"I did feel pretty invincible, baby," Kyree returned the gesture by wrapping his own arm around Ambrose's waist, adding his own twist by giving his lover's ass a swift caress.

"Kyree Landon, do not grope me in front of our daughter," Ambrose scolded playfully, leaning in close and catching Kyree's earlobe between his perfect teeth, "not that I don't love your hands all over me," Ambrose purred, a smirk on his lips.

"Ew, dads, stop," the playful nature between the two men dissipated instantly at one little word in Saige's sentence. Their gazes both snapped to her, startled eyes meeting nervous ones that averted instantly to the floor.

"You've never called us that before," Kyree marvelled, observing Saige's sudden fidgety behaviour.

"Sorry, it just slipped out," she murmured, her cheeks flushed and her lip caught between her teeth. Kyree exchanged a compassionate smile with Ambrose.

"Let it slip more often, my dear," Saige looked up, her emerald eyes somehow lighting up more than they already were, sharing in the two men's smiles.

"OK, anyway, I came down to wake you because Lucifer wants breakfast with us all, he wants to talk about tomorrow night," Kyree's brows furrowed in a bemused manner.

"Tomorrow night?"

"Coronation," Ambrose groaned, pinching the bridge of his nose as the stress headache that had plagued him for the last month weaselled its way back into his mind, "I completely forget with everything that was going on with your trial and now this. God, I haven't even got a suit for you since..." Ambrose trailed off, obviously not wanting to relive the fact that his lover was almost taken from him the previous night.

"Can't you postpone it?"

"A demonic coronation can only occur during a lunar eclipse in the winter equinox. Either I get coronated tomorrow night or my sister takes my place and I don't get the opportunity for another 3 millennia," Ambrose took a deep breath, forcing a smile on his lips, "Saige, honey, can you go tell my father we will join him within the hour? Can you also ask him to book the tailor for tomorrow morning, for Kyree?" Saige nodded, her usual soft smile taking it's seat on her mouth.

"Don't be late, dads," she added as she brisked out of the door, closing it gently behind her. Ambrose turned his attention back to Kyree, an innocent little smirk on his lips.

"Still want that shower?"

"Azazel?" Kyree suggested, striding hand in hand down the hallway with his lover, "means fallen angel," Ambrose tipped his head side to side, silently debating the name. The hallway in the royal palace was beautiful. Stark white marble columns either side, paintings from various eras littering the walls, golden carpets somehow so clean they looked as though they were shimmering.

"Also means sacrificial offering, I don't like to think of it as a sacrifice. I mean, we surrender independence for unity but I see that as a gain rather than a sacrifice," Kyree nodded, pushing open the door that Ambrose had led him to. Kyree's eyes widened as the two men entered the grand dining room, all eyes latching onto them. Lucifer was sat at the head of a relatively large table, with a younger woman to his right and Saige three seats down to his left.

"Sorry, are we late, father?" Ambrose asked politely, pecking a chaste kiss on Kyree's cheek as his chair was pulled out from him. Once Ambrose was seated, Kyree took the seat next to him, flashing a soft smile at Saige.

"Not at all, Ambrose," Lucifer smiled at his son, his successor, "did you both sleep well?" Kyree couldn't help the slight snort of laughter than bubbled within him. They might have slept well if they had slept at all but, of course, a month apart left both of them aching for one another's touch.

"In a sense, yes," Ambrose replied, ambiguity at its finest, giving Kyree's hand a soft squeeze, careful not to extend the contact between the brand for too long in case their power decided to act up again.

"Kyree, I don't believe you have met my daughter. This is Essence," the young woman sat next to Lucifer flashed a bashful smile toward Kyree. She had long dark hair, the same hue as Ambrose's, and deep brown eyes. Her lips had the same fullness as Ambrose's, but she pouted too much, didn't hold her posture with the confidence of her elder brother either. She seemed like a meek version of Ambrose.

"Nice to meet you," she murmured, barely having the courage to look Kyree in the eye.

"You too," Kyree responded politely, detecting a wisp of irritation from Ambrose as he saw the frown curl on his lover's face in his peripheral vision. The five began eating, Lucifer having some hushed conversation with Essence, giving Kyree and Ambrose the opportunity to continue theirs from earlier.

"What about Samael?" Ambrose offered, catching Kyree's subtly drifting attention, "he was the grim reaper, accuser and destroyer. He was chief seducer as well, perfectly describes you," Kyree chuckled at Ambrose's absurd comment.

"Are you having a kid?" Saige interjected suddenly, her voice just loud enough to unintentionally catch the attention of Lucifer and Essence. Upon noticing her mistake, she grimaced, apologising softly.

"No, my dear, we are not having a child," Kyree ran his fingers down her arm, smiling tenderly, "we are trying to name the creature that appears when our brands touch, we can't just call it 'the creature' now, can we?"

"Oh, have you thought about Abigor?" Ambrose clicked his tongue softly as Saige's suggestion.

"Hmm, I've heard that name somewhere," he murmured distantly, lost in thought.

"He was the ruler of 60 legions in Hell, and a knight," Saige shrugged, simpering at the shocked expressions of the people around her, "I did a lot of religious theology in school."

"He was also one of the few handsome demons," Essence chimed in, staring innocently through her dark lashes at Kyree, that same lustrous look that he adored on Ambrose didn't look nearly as appealing on her slight face. Kyree actually caught an audible growl from Ambrose, noting the tension in the air between the two siblings.

"How many times have you shifted into this creature? This... Abigor?" Lucifer tried out the new name given for the creature, it sounded right rolling of the Ruler's tongue, menacing even, just what Kyree had hoped for.

"Once, earlier this morning. We don't know how to control it yet but it happened when our brands touched so we're assuming that contact triggers it," Kyree explained, keeping an eye on Ambrose as he glared daggers at his sister.

"Ky? When it happened, did your brand glow?" Saige quavered, her eyes fixed on the growing amber glow emanating from the brands on Ambrose and Kyree's arms. Kyree glanced down at his bare arm, the sleeve rolled up, cursing under his breath.

"Ambrose, we should-" Kyree didn't have time finish his sentence before Abigor stood in his place, the chairs he and Ambrose had been sitting on clattering back against the wooden floorboards.

"My God, he's beautiful," Essence breathed, her eyes wide, flittering all over Abigor's features. She would have marvelled, would have basked in the glow of amber from Abigor's slow pumping veins, if Abigor had calmed and listened to Kyree's whispers that is.

Instead, the creature appeared next to Essence, wrenching her from her seat by her tiny throat, slamming her petite body into the wall behind them. Her feet dangled, just barely grazing against the golden carpet as she gasped for breath, squirming in Abigor's iron grip.

"You're a slut," Abigor growled, his apathetic, colourless eyes latched onto hers as she struggled for air, "you always have been. Always wanting what you can't have. Always ruining his happiness," Kyree's whispers had grown to all-out screaming, his shouts pounding against the walls of Abigor's skull.

Abigor was not Kyree, and he was not Ambrose. He was a mixture of them both, a completely different personality. He was swayed by their emotions, taking orders from them no matter what. But when they fought, God it was agony when they fought. Each clutching at the control of the beast, their opposing thoughts and emotions ripping Abigor apart inside.

"Abigor, stop!" Saige's voice tore through Abigor's anger, the fury that was being fuelled by Ambrose, "please, you're scaring me," she sounded so frail, her voice trembling as she moved into view at his right. Abigor's large, char coloured eyes landed on her, immediately noting the fear in her pale face. The anger from Ambrose ceased, as did the desperation from Kyree.

Relief flooded the beast, his Master's were agreeing, both equally appalled at scaring their daughter. Abigor understood his place, understood he was no longer needed at that moment. Releasing Essence from his grip, and feeling some form of satisfaction from her whimper as her almost limp body hit the floor with a soft thud, Abigor returned to his dwelling in his Master's bond. Their separate bodies took his place and he nuzzled back into their brands, awaiting the next time he would be awakened.

Chapter 22

"Ow! Fuck! Stick me with one more pin and I'll-"

"Kyree," Ambrose clasped his lover's hand from behind, shaking his head gently with a smile on his lips, "don't be rude," Kyree scowled at Ambrose but did as he said and stayed quiet for the remainder of the fitting with the tailor.

"I am finished, my Lord," the tailor rose to his feet, ensuring to keep his eyes on the carpet for fear of making eye contact with his soon to be king. The tailor had already been late, due to the high security for the coronation later that evening, so had tried his best to work fast.

Kyree stepped down from the podium, striding over to the full-length mirror, Ambrose following at his heel with a grin on his face. His suit was that same beautiful shade of obsidian as Ambrose's horns, Kyree's new favourite colour. The fabric shimmered in the light, just as Ambrose's horns did.

"You like it, baby?" Ambrose purred in Kyree's ear, "I picked the colour out just for you, remembered how much you like it on me," Kyree groaned as

Ambrose caught his earlobe between his teeth, biting down hard enough that he knew there would be a mark.

"Out," Kyree demanded the tailor, pleased with how fast the little man scuttled from the room. The second Kyree heard the door click shut, he pressed Ambrose against the wall to the left of them, covering his mouth with his own. Ambrose complied with a soft moan and a tug of Kyree's hair, his other hand clutching the lapel of Kyree's suit, as if holding himself up for fear his knees may buckle.

Kyree's mouth trailed down Ambrose's neck, leaving one deep purple bruise after another across his demon's tanned skin. Ambrose's mewls and purrs were loud, then again, Ambrose always was loud, he knew it turned Kyree on. Kyree was marking his lover, knowing that all eyes would be on them tonight, he wanted everyone to know what was his.

"Mine," he murmured against Ambrose's abused flesh, nipping at the place just below his lover's jaw, marvelling in the primal groan that resonated through him.

"Yours," Ambrose agreed, his chest heaving as his breath got taken from him by another quick nip across his throat from Kyree, "forever, baby," Kyree took a step back, admiring the myriad of mauve marks littered across Ambrose's throat. Purple was Kyree's favourite colour on Ambrose.

"You're really gonna just stop?" Ambrose almost whined, reaching out in an attempt to tug Kyree back into his arms, "got me all worked up for nothing, baby?" Ambrose pouted, making his already full, raw lips look somehow more luscious.

"And what would you want me to do?" Kyree straightened his suit jacket, cocking an eyebrow as he watched Ambrose, "my king?" Ambrose's eyes glowed a deep black, a smirk tugging at the corners of his mouth.

"Well, it is gonna be such a long night, baby," Ambrose closed the distance between him and his lover, "and no doubt you'll be swaying your ass all night, just tempting me," Ambrose purred seductively, his lustful gaze intent on Kyree.

"Shit, I'm interrupting again, aren't I?" Saige's voice drifted into the room, "sorry, dads, I'll come back," Kyree chuckled softly, shaking his head gently.

"You do have impeccably inopportune timing, my dear," Kyree turned, smiling as Ambrose's arms snaked around his hips from behind, holding him against the demon, "what did you need?"

"Luci's getting restless, he says it's only an hour before the coronation and he hasn't seen either of you yet. So he sent me, as usual," Ambrose tittered quietly behind Kyree, resting his chin on his lover's shoulder.

"I have never heard anyone call my father Luci, he is your grandfather, you know, you can address him as that if you wish."

"I like Luci, grandfather is way too formal. Anyway, don't change the subject, get dressed before he spontaneously combusts," Ambrose smiled at his daughter, she may not have been Kyree's blood but she sure as hell acted as if she were.

"You too, honey, tell him we'll be no longer than ten minutes," as Saige exited the room, Ambrose let go of Kyree, striding over to the wardrobe.

"Tell me again, how does this coronation work?" Kyree was overly nervous, and he wasn't even truly being crowned. Until they married, Kyree would only be a prince. He would be more of an advisor whilst he was in that position, then when they decided to marry he would gain a lot more control and their wedding day would act as Kyree's coronation.

Ambrose had given him the option of marrying the same day as the coronation but Kyree wasn't ready for that. It wasn't that he didn't love Ambrose, or that he didn't want to spend the rest of his eternal life with him. It was the fear that their wedding could have the same unhappy ending as Kyree had with Alexander. He couldn't bear that, silently hoping that if they just never married the threat and fear would dwindle within him.

"You don't have much to do, baby," Ambrose reassured, shedding his clothing and dressing in his suit. It was similar to the one that Kyree had worn for his trial. The subtle silver inlay had a soft reddish tinge to it, glistening in the light as Ambrose moved.

"After I have been crowned, you merely pledge an oath to me. The people have yet to find out about us, only my father's closest friends and colleagues have been told. Hopefully, they should take our companionship well."

"And what about Saige?"

"She will pledge the oath too," Ambrose caught sight of Kyree's pale and nervous stare, "baby, you're gonna be fine, OK? Everything is gonna go fine," Ambrose cupped Kyree's cheek, tipping his head up so their eyes locked. Ambrose had always loved Kyree's hazel eyes, but having one of his grey-blue iris' in his lover somehow looked so much better.

"What about the assassin? Surely he's gonna be there. And what if we lose control? What if we summon Abigor?" Kyree was babbling, his sheer terror consuming him with every passing moment.

"The security is higher than it's ever been, baby, he won't be able to get in. No one can use their powers in the coronation hall, the bricks are laced with devil's snare," devil's snare, also known as Datura stramonium, the one plant in the entire human or underworld that could inhibit a demon's powers. The assassin used it in every one of his murder attempts, which was why they took so long to heal from.

"I don't know, Amb, I can't help but feel this is all just a bad idea. I mean, I wish you could postpone this until we found the assassin, you being so out in the open would be such an easy for him to-" Ambrose shut Kyree up by pressing a gentle kiss to his lips, rubbing his thumb over Kyree's cheekbone.

"Calm, baby, you need to stay calm. We're all gonna be fine, I promise."

The coronation hall was most definitely grand. Simply the doorway leading into it had such beautiful craftsmanship Kyree wondered how it was that someone like him was to enter. He had simply wanted to be Ambrose's knight, yet now he was being crowned as a prince. It still felt so surreal.

"Baby?" Ambrose's voice roused Kyree from his thoughts.

"Hmm?" Kyree made eye contact with his lover, a weak smile on his lips.

"I asked if you were OK, you looked distant," Kyree let out a breath, ignoring the trembling in his hands.

"Being like this, waiting to walk down an aisle to the man I love. I can't help noticing the similarities of a wedding," Kyree admitted, worry in his heterochromic eyes, "just don't leave, OK? Please, don't leave my side before you have to," Ambrose smiled tenderly, pressing a chaste kiss to Kyree's lips.

"I have nowhere to go, I am exactly where I am supposed to be," the chatter from the hall was growing louder, indicative of restless demons awaiting the crowning of their new king.

"Ready?" Saige piped up, stepping next to Kyree. She looked breathtaking in her deep black gown. It was sheer and short in the middle, with black flowers littered over the material. Yet there was a more opaque fabric around it similar to a coat. It sat tightly up Saige's arms and tied in the middle of her stomach before flowing loosely down to the floor, leaving her legs to be viewed by all.

"You look radiant, my dear," Kyree murmured, kissing her lilac hair before linking her arm with his. Ambrose was to go first, to enter alone prior to Kyree and Saige. It would then be obvious to the people that Kyree was to be crowned too, if only as a prince.

With the flash of a compassionate smile to his lover, Ambrose set off into the hall, feeling the weakening effect of the devil's snare the second he set foot into the room. Silence reigned as he strode smoothly down the aisle toward his father stood at the opposite end. All eyes were on him, demon men and women alike drinking in his striking appearance.

When he took his place at the end of the aisle, glancing back toward the door, awaiting Kyree and Saige's entrance, the demon felt his chest tightening. Flashes of that fateful day echoed through Kyree's mind, the day that was supposed to bring him such joy but instead haunted him relentlessly.

Images in front of Kyree's eyes seemed to swim as he tried desperately to calm himself enough to take a breath. He was trembling, his entire body wracked with tremors as he simply stared fearfully at the aisle he should have already been walking down.

"Dad? Ky, what's wrong?" Saige questioned gingerly the second she felt Kyree's grip tighten. Kyree could sense the bemusement of everyone around him. Saige wondering why they weren't moving, the demons in the hall wondering why the ceremony hadn't begun and, most of all, Ambrose wondering if Kyree had left him.

That thought struck him the hardest, like a slap across the face. He couldn't do that to Ambrose, wouldn't do that. He knew what it was like to be left there, at an altar, be it a wedding or otherwise, just simply to be left waiting on the one you love only to have them never appear.

"Don't let go," Kyree muttered to Saige, slipping his hand into hers rather than having his arm linked with hers. The first step was the hardest, the dulling effect of the devil's snare slowing his movements just a little. Yet, he felt such strength as he saw Ambrose's face light up at the sight of him.

Soft gasps echoed through the room from the demons. Maybe it was from people who knew Kyree, or maybe others were just surprised by the entrance of Kyree and his daughter. Yet no one spoke, simply observed as Kyree made his way to his position next to Ambrose.

"I was worried there for a second," Ambrose whispered, "thought you weren't coming," Kyree slipped his free hand into Ambrose's, caressing the back of his knuckles.

"I would never leave you like that, I love you too much."

Chapter 23

The coronation began with every previously standing demon in the hall taking their seat. Lucifer smiled vehemently down at his son, also including Kyree and Saige in his proud gaze. With a soft kiss to the back of Ambrose's hand, Kyree stepped to the side with Saige, leaving Ambrose alone centre stage, their presence not needed until later.

"Today is a day that shall be remembered for centuries, even millennia to come," Lucifer began, his thunderous voice echoing through the hall, "today, Hell crowns a new king. A new generation is brought into royalty, into power in our world, ushering our people into a new age. Ambrose Ross," Ambrose dropped to one knee silently in front of his father, his Lord, his head bowed in deference, "my son, my heir, my successor. Soon to be even my king," Kyree allowed his gaze to wander through the crowd seated with their full attention on Ambrose and his father. Along the front row of seats to the right was Essence, Deacon and another man Kyree had never met nor even recognised. To the left were Yennifer, Orion and Idella. Kyree's parents looked immensely proud, Kyree could even detect a tear welling his father's eye.

"Ambrose Zagan Ross," Kyree suppressed a snigger at the first mention of Ambrose's middle name, "do you pledge to forever put the needs of Hell first? Before blood, before love and before happiness? Do you pledge your allegiance to the people of Hell, the demons that you will rule and any others who choose to take refuge in this realm?"

"Yes, father, I do. I vow to do everything in my will to protect and serve those under my power," Ambrose may have directed his speech to the immaculate burgundy carpet he was knelt on but Kyree knew every demon in Hell somehow heard that oath loud and clear.

Kyree's lips parted ever so slightly in a silent gasp as two thick black horns grew from Lucifer's head. They were almost identical in the pearlescent obsidian shade that coated them, but Lucifer's were longer and thicker, curved in a sense that was similar to Abigor's.

What truly made them stand out to Kyree, though, was the flecks of silver littered through them black, as if laced into the design after it had already been crafted. Ambrose's hair parted as his own pair of horns sprouted from his head, although Kyree had no idea how he had known to do it in that moment since his eyes had remained on the floor during the entire speech.

"Stand, my child," Lucifer commanded, all eyes on Ambrose as he rose to his feet, finally making eye contact with his father. Lucifer removed a simple golden ring from his right hand, slipping it onto Ambrose's right finger on his respective hand.

"We do not wear crowns in this world, my child, for we are all equals. This ring has been passed down through our bloodline from king to prince for generations. It is a symbol of strength in simplicity. And as my final gift to my eldest child, I bestow upon you the gifts of royalty in this world," Ambrose made no hesitation in gripping his father's outstretched hand with his own, a pained grimace plastered across his face the second their skin made contact.

Kyree was glad Saige had heeded his warning and kept a hold of his hand as she was the only thing preventing him from some outburst at the suffering Lucifer had called a gift. It was a few seconds before Kyree truly noticed it, Ambrose's horns were growing. They were lengthening, the tips curling as flecks of silver seemed to bubble to the beautiful black surface of them.

As Ambrose's power built, his father's dwindled. If Kyree had thought Ambrose was suffering, Lucifer was in agony, a bead of sweat forming on his brow as he forced himself to keep his eyes locked with his son. His horns withered, dulling from that bewitching black to steely, matted shade of silver.

Sensing that the transfer of power was almost through, Kyree dared to take a step closer to the two demons. As Kyree had anticipated, when the physical contact broke between Lucifer and his son, the elder man stumbled backwards lightly, caught by Kyree's hand resting on his back.

"Thank you, Kyree," Lucifer muttered gratefully, composing himself as Kyree nodded curtly, his gaze drifting to Ambrose. A small smile turned up the corners of Kyree's mouth as a shimmer of silver flickered through Ambrose's darkened eyes.

"Sexy," Kyree mouthed with a wink, putting a matching smile on Ambrose's lips.

"I can sense that many of you wonder why Ambrose had been accompanied by two others when not a word of any sort of partnership has been spoken since my son's engagement to Deacon Rome," with a subtle tilt of his head, Kyree motioned for Saige to step forward, anticipating their looming involvement in the ceremony, "Kyree Landon, previously training for the position as Ambrose's knight, chose instead to stand by his side as his lover. Saige Landon, turned just last month by Kyree, has been taken as their child, their daughter," Saige beamed at her father's, tears in her emerald eyes. Remembering the instructions they had been given, Saige and Kyree dropped to one knee simultaneously as Ambrose had done before them.

"Kyree Landon, do you pledge your allegiance, your fealty, to your King Ambrose Ross? Do you vow to remain by his side with unwavering loyalty through his reign, no matter the status of the relationship between the two of you?"

"I do," Kyree spoke with a tone of complete sincerity, a serious expression on his averted gaze.

"And Saige Landon, do you take an oath of fidelity to, not only your fathers, but to your kings? Do you, despite your brief time in this world, promise to devote your eternal life to upholding the reputation of the family and bloodline you are brought into on this day?" Saige was hesitant for a second but agreed nonetheless as she had been advised to do earlier that day.

Lucifer produced a long silver dagger from thin air. The handle sparkled with red flecks of shimmering material over the black and worn leather. Rolling up his sleeve, Ambrose held out his wrist, allowing his father to drag the blade over his tanned skin, cutting through a few layers of flesh with ease.

Despite having been told that Kyree would have been the first to have been given Ambrose's blood, Ambrose chose to step over to Saige first, tipping her head back gently. Her lips barely parted, her mouth only open ever so slightly as Ambrose's deep red blood dripped down into it. She grimaced at the taste, returning her head to the same bowed position the second she felt his hand removed from her hair.

Ambrose ran the fingers of his other hand through Kyree's brunette locks, urging him to tip his head back and finally look up at his lover. Ambrose had no emotion in his face, not even a flicker of empathy for Kyree to savour. Then again, Kyree had expected and been warned that Ambrose would act that way. Didn't make the experience any less daunting though.

Kyree opened his mouth as he had been instructed, waiting to hear the soft patter of the blood hitting his tongue. Yet, it didn't come. Instead, he watched as Ambrose lifted his wrist to his mouth and allowed the blood to pool in his mouth, his eyes never once leaving Kyree's even as a soft chorus of gasps and mutterings rippled through the crowd.

Kyree's brows drew together in a bemused frown until Ambrose took a knee in front of him, covering his mouth with his own. Ambrose's lips tasted as they usually did, intoxicating and sweet, yet it was mixed with the bitter, metallic taste of his blood. Kyree suppressed a groan as Ambrose's tongue invaded his mouth, stroking against every inch of his warm, wet flesh, the remaining blood seeping through.

When Ambrose finally broke the kiss, both men were just a little breathless. Kyree ran his thumb over Ambrose's bottom lip, that was now curved into a wicked smirk, collecting the final drop of blood before bringing it to his mouth and gladly flicking his tongue over it.

Maybe Kyree would have said something, maybe Ambrose would, had Saige not suddenly doubled over in pain, clutching at her head. Ambrose moved to her side quickly, manoeuvring her so she was sat, still on the floor, facing away from the crowd, whimpering softly as he held her.

Kyree felt the piercing agony rupture his skull also, but was trying desperately to refrain from crying out, choosing instead to clench his jaw and ball his hands into fists so tight his knuckles turned stark white. Ambrose glanced over at him, a flicker of worry on his face, but Kyree merely waved his concern away with a small, forced smile.

Saige whined quietly as two horns grew gradually from her head, parting the beautiful lilac hair. Kyree could feel the same happening to him as he watched his daughter suffer. Ambrose was whispering to her, hopefully something about being strong and how the pain would only occur for so long.

It took minutes before the sensation finally subsided and Saige glanced over at Kyree. He did not know what his own horns looked like but he assumed they were the same as Saige's, identical to what Ambrose's had been before the power transfer. The bewitching shade of obsidian glimmering in the dim lighting of the coronation hall.

Ambrose helped Saige to her feet, then Kyree, stood between them both to ensure neither toppled from the pain. The demons observing them were silent, staring with wide eyes at the display they had just watched. Kyree did not know what to do as the seconds past and no sound was made. That was until Saige stepped forward, a grin on her lips.

"Long live the kings!" she called out, the first crack to break the dam. Cheers and applause roared through the coronation hall as the demons stood, finally revealing their true feelings about the new royalty. Ambrose snaked an arm around Kyree's waist, chuckling softly as Saige stepped back, wrapping her arms around her fathers.

"Well, that went much better than expected."

Chapter 24

"Ah ah ah, you're underage," Ambrose lifted the wine glass from Saige, a smug smile on his lips as she pouted.

"Oh, come on, dad, please?" she whined, "Ky lets me," Ambrose clicked his tongue softly, glancing over at Kyree who was stood talking with his brother across the room. As they made eye contact, a smile took over Kyree's face and he politely excused himself from his conversation and strode over.

"Is it true you have been letting our 16-year-old daughter drink?" Ambrose asked in feigned anger, merely causing Kyree to chuckle.

"I was doing much worse at her age, babe, a little alcohol here and there never hurt anyone," Saige had that same smug smirk Kyree adorned when he knew he was winning an argument and Ambrose wondered how they acted so alike despite not truly being related.

"And what was it you were doing at 16 that was so terrible?" Kyree chuckled once again, leaning forward and whispering in Ambrose's ear. He obscured the demon's view, slipping the wine glass from his hand and holding it behind his back for Saige to take. Without a word, she withdrew the glass from his hand, gliding away into the masses of the ballroom.

"You are not allowed to gang up on me until we have another child that can take my side," Ambrose scolded, laughing at Kyree and Saige's cunning little display.

"You want more children then? You don't think Saige is a handful enough?" Kyree asked, sipping from his own glass of wine.

"I always wanted a big family, baby, never thought I would get one though," Ambrose cupped Kyree's cheek, a warm smile on his lips, "you gave me the one thing I desired most, a daughter. I would love to return that favour," Kyree placed his hand over Ambrose's, returning the warm smile.

"I love you," Kyree uttered, his eyes latched onto Ambrose's.

"I love you too," that small gesture between the two somehow led them onto the dancefloor. A slow song, one that was melancholy yet set an air of blissful optimism played as the two danced, held in each other's arms.

Kyree enjoyed the feeling of his head rested against Ambrose's as their bodies swayed together to the beat of the music filling the room. It was as if they were the only two in the room, as if they held the entire world in their arms clasped around each other. How very cliche of it all.

Not too long into the song, Kyree felt someone tap his shoulder, bringing his consciousness rushing back down earth from that other plain he often drifted too when alone with Ambrose. Tilting his head and, consequently alerting Ambrose that they were no longer alone with their thoughts, Kyree saw Saige stood nervously behind him.

"What is it, my dear? Something the matter?" Kyree queried gingerly, a small stroke of worry setting into him.

"No, nothing. Actually, everything seems so perfect I thought this was a pretty good time to tell you I'm seeing someone," Saige reached behind her, tugging the arm of a man close by, urging him to turn. As the man's face came into view, Kyree felt anger, rage even, swell within him, consuming his mind, body and soul like wildfire spreading through a drought-filled forest.

"Dads, this is Tyrell Kaine, my- oh my God," Saige gasped as the wine glass in Kyree's hand shattered, sending blood, wine and glass cascading to the floor. Kyree ignored the pain of his horns growing, most of it drowned out by the anger fuelled purely by the sight of Tyrell's face.

"You," he seethed, his eyes seeping to a deep black, glowering at Tyrell, who merely looked on innocently. People were staring, silencing themselves to watch Kyree's outburst.

"No, Kyree," Ambrose hissed, gripping Kyree's wrist so tight he actually felt the bruise forming, "not here, outside, now. All of you," he command-ed, dragging Kyree out with Saige and Tyrell following at their heel, not daring to disobey their king. The second they were in the hallway, out of sight from prying eyes, Kyree's bloodied fist came into contact with Tyrell's jaw, sending him stumbling backwards.

"Dad!" Saige shrieked, holding Tyrell as he clutched his jaw, standing be-tween her boyfriend and her father, "what the fuck is wrong with you?!" Kyree moved to hit Tyrell again but Ambrose caught his fist, his own eyes dark as the night as he scowled at his lover.

"Calm down, Kyree," he seethed, his voice low and emotionless, "right fucking now," keeping his own char coloured eyes locked with Ambrose's, Kyree took a few laboured breaths, "good, now open your hand and let me get the glass out before you heal around it," Kyree presented his upturned palm to Ambrose, grimacing as his lover plucked pieces of glass from his torn skin.

"Will somebody please tell me what is going on?" Saige's voice shook, either with fear or anger, Ambrose could not tell. He glanced at Kyree as he removed the glass, who was still glowering at Tyrell.

"Saige," Kyree spoke before Ambrose could, "you can be with anyone. And I mean anyone. Male, female, fucking unicorn for all I care. But not him. Not Tyrell Kaine," Kyree growled.

"Why?" Kyree averted his eyes to Ambrose, who was examining the bruise he had given Kyree when dragging him from the ballroom, "Kyree, tell me why," Saige demanded, more force in her tone that time.

"Saige, your father has a deep and darkened history with Tyrell. He is not a good man, he is a plague. I assumed the last time we met he would have gotten the hint that he is not welcome here. Clearly not," Tyrell scoffed at Ambrose's comment, rolling his eyes.

"You mean when you beat me within an inch of my life for simply wishing Kyree a happy birthday?" Saige looked appalled at the revelation of Ambrose's more malicious side. To her, he was kind and gentle, yet she suddenly had a new aspect of him to factor into her image of her father.

"You deserved it, don't act like you didn't provoke me. Kyree had already warned you of what would happen should you show your face again but you just didn't listen. I don't regret what I did to you, not in the slightest. In fact, maybe I should have gotten a few more kicks in before Kyree found us. Then our little problem here would not have been an issue," Ambrose spat, feeling the anger from Kyree ever so slowly awakening Abigor.

"Ambrose," Saige whispered, fear and disappointment mixed into her expression, "I've never heard you say something so heartless."

"We're demons, Saige, we are heartless. We have compassion only for those who deserve it. He does not."

"You say that, but you have still yet to give me any reason to distrust him. Tyrell has been nothing but a perfect gentleman to me and I... I really like him," Saige slipped a hand into Tyrell's, flashing him a weak smile before returning her stony expression to her fathers.

"Kyree was engaged to his brother, Saige. Alexander was tortured and hung by humans on their wedding day 5 years ago. Tyrell blames Kyree, taunts him with it, which is why he is not welcome here. He is more spiteful and callous than you know," oddly, Tyrell laughed bitterly, shaking his head.

"Of course he would tell you that story, that makes him sound more like the dragon slayer than the dragon itself."

"What are you talking about?"

"Oh Ambrose, so easily swayed by the words of a grieving man. I do not blame Kyree because of the actions he told you that lead up to my brother's death. That story is utter shit. Kyree was not a factor in Alexander's death, he was the cause. He murdered him, with his two hands," Kyree lunged at Tyrell but Ambrose held him back, just barely, so that Saige would not be caught in the crossfire.

"How dare you! How dare you accuse me of something like that! I loved him! Why the hell would I kill him?!" Kyree roared, emotion pouring from him into the brand, the deep amber glow beginning to build. Ambrose focused on forcing Abigor away, he didn't need another rage-fuelled beast adding to the explosive situation.

"Because he was having an affair!" Kyree stilled, his body so motionless it was as if he was dead on his feet, "he fell in love with a human man, went to him on the morning of the wedding because he wanted to be with him, not Kyree. Kyree found them together and lost his temper, though that phrase does not do justice to what he anger he unleashed on my poor brother. Then, not wanting to be seen as the culprit, he strung my brother up like some doll and acted as though he had just found him there. If I'm such a terrible man, there are no words for what Kyree is," Tyrell retorted, venom in his tone yet smouldering triumph in his eyes. Kyree's chest heaved as he tried desperately to control his breathing, his body trembling with anger and something else... guilt maybe?

It was the look Saige gave him that sent him over the edge. Tearing himself from Ambrose's grasp, Kyree took the stairs two at a time, needing to be away from anyone and everyone. Ambrose watched him go with sorrowful eyes, then looked at Saige and Tyrell, shaking his head gently.

"Still think he's such a gentleman?" Ambrose muttered, shouldering past his stunned daughter as he followed Kyree upstairs. Presumably, Kyree had retreated to their bedroom, and if the sounds of pacing and occasionally something being broken were any indication, Ambrose was correct.

"Ky? Baby?" Ambrose kept his voice soft as he entered their bedroom, seeing Kyree sat on the edge of the bed with his head hung in his hands, "oh, baby, are you OK?" Ambrose perched next to Kyree, rubbing small circles on his lover's back, coaxing him to look toward him. When Kyree did finally lift his head, his eyes were red and puffy and tears stained his cheeks.

"I didn't kill him," he whispered weakly, "how could I think I killed him, Amb? He wasn't there, where did he get this idea?"

"I don't know, baby, I don't know," the two sat in silence for a few seconds, before Kyree took a deep breath, forcing a lopsided smile onto his trembling lips.

"You need to get back to your guests, babe, I'll be down in five," Ambrose shook his head, not convinced Kyree was in the slightest better.

"They can wait, I'm not leaving you right now."

"Ambrose," Kyree rose to his feet, pressing a kiss to Ambrose's forehead, "please, I'll be down in five, I promise," Kyree insisted, tugging Ambrose to his feet gently, "go, mingle, I just need to freshen up and I'll join you, OK?"

"Mmm OK," Ambrose caved, an unsure smile on his lips, "five minutes then I'm coming up to find you, baby," with a chaste kiss, Ambrose left Kyree, closing the door behind him. Kyree spent a few minutes staring out the window, up at the starless sky, simply lost in thought. That was, until he heard the door open.

"Babe, it's only been three minutes, I'm fine," Kyree glanced over his shoulder, seeing a figure stood next to the door, it's face covered by shadows, "Ambrose? What are you doing?" a low chuckle resonated through the room, setting an ominous tension through the air.

"If only I were Ambrose, my troubles would all be gone," a deep, distorted voice spoke, the sound easily carried through the room to Kyree's ears.

"Who are you?"

"Wouldn't you like to know," the figure spoke with a menacing chuckle, "but if I told you it would make our little game redundant, and I do enjoy playing with you and Ambrose."

"Let me guess, you're the assassin?" Kyree spoke as realisation dawned on him, Ambrose had mentioned he had gotten more brazen. That was an understatement.

"In the flesh," the figure held out his arms as if showing off his presence, "and at a perfect time as well, I do love to feed off your agony. It seems to be emanating from you tonight," there was at least a 10-foot distance between Kyree and the assassin, one that he would not be able to cross in time without the figure attempting something. Fear flooded Kyree as he remembered Ambrose would be back to check on him soon, he couldn't have him hurt. He couldn't stall, he simply had to act.

"So, you're here to kill me?" the assassin answered with a simple nod and Kyree knew he had a smirk on his mouth, "take your best sh-" Kyree's sentence was cut off by the sudden jolt of piercing agony through his back. The figure by the door dissipated into a wisp of smoke, it was a decoy. He felt a hand on his hip holding him upright, another on his mouth to prevent him from calling out for help.

"Kyree, I didn't have a name for you before today," a voice whispered in his ear as the dagger was twisted in his back, coaxing a strangled groan from him, "but after hearing that precious story of how you murdered your own fiance, it came to me. You, Kyree Landon, are a black dog. A death omen."

Chapter 25

Panic began to set in as Kyree struggled with taking a breath, a simple action that was ingrained into his brain yet couldn't be called upon in that moment. He had been injured before, for God sake he had been shot, but somehow the feeling of the cold, serrated metal plunging into his flesh was so much worse.

"No witty retort, Kyree? Cat got your tongue?" the assassin mocked, humour in his tone. He was enjoying Kyree suffering, probably getting off on it too. Kyree tried to speak but only managed a choked gurgling sound, probably from the blood seeping into his lungs and airway.

His body was growing heavier by the minute, the sound of his blood dripping onto the carpet growing more and more distant. He was going to pass out. He was going to die. No. No, that couldn't happen. He couldn't die, he wouldn't leave Ambrose like that.

Mustering what little strength dwindled within him, Kyree launched himself forward, managing a few steps before collapsing half onto the bed with a cry of pain. A low throaty laugh filled his ears, along with an awful buzzing that seemed to be growing as he drifted further and further from consciousness.

A hand clamped over his mouth, just as another pressed roughly into the gaping wound in his back, causing him to almost scream from the pain. Colours were swimming in front of his eyes, the world tipping and tilting as fingers probed the inner walls of the wound, inciting a burning and aching sensation Kyree had never experienced before.

"Can't you just fucking die already?" the voice hissed in Kyree's ear as he felt the blade plunge into another patch of flesh in his back. He wasn't even able to produce any noise that time, simply blinked as another wave of agony crashed over him.

Suddenly, Kyree's head was filled with the sound of growling and snarling. He tried desperately to focus on the black mass stood in the doorway, hunched over and growing gradually. The hand over his mouth slipped away, in fact, the pressure of any presence near him seemed to drift as the growling got louder.

"Good dog..." Kyree muttered his praise as he forced himself to his feet and stumbled blindly from the room, praying to every God he had ever heard of that his damn dog wouldn't get killed. The stairs were difficult, for some reason Kyree kept scolding himself mentally for getting blood everywhere, as though that was truly the most important thought at that moment.

He struggled with the door, his blood making the handle slippy and difficult to push down. He finally managed it when another wave of pain hit, bringing tears to his eyes. Not physical pain, no, that had never stopped. It was emotional, it was the fear of losing Ambrose, of leaving him as Alexander had left Kyree. He couldn't bear that, and that gave him strength.

The door swung open easily and Kyree took maybe two steps before dropping to his knees, his eyes half closed. Screams filled the ballroom as people saw Kyree, backing away from him, staring rather than helping.

Ambrose heard the commotion, elbowed his way to the front of the crowd. If his heart had been beating, it would have stopped in that moment. The sight of his lover, his Kyree, drenched with blood, eyes dull as his body swayed on the precipice of unconsciousness. It could have killed Ambrose easily.

"Kyree!" he yelled, dropping his wine glass and running to catch Kyree just as his lover fell backwards, "Ky, baby, stay with me. OK? Keep your eyes open," Ambrose felt along Kyree's back, finding two rather large stab wounds that were gushing blood, only able to hold one shut.

"Oh my God, dad!" Saige almost sprinted over as she caught sight of her two father's, tears already streaming down her cheeks, "Ambrose, what happened?" she quavered, clutching Kyree's bloodied hand with her own trembling ones.

"He's been stabbed," Ambrose said bluntly, his eyes wild with fear, "Saige, give me your hand, you need to hold one shut whilst he starts to heal," Ambrose tugged Saige's hand under Kyree, pressing it against one of the wounds, "hold it tight, he can't lose anymore blood," Kyree stared up at the ceiling with a dazed expression on his face, he wasn't sure he had any more blood to lose.

"D-Dog..." he stammered weakly, catching Ambrose's attention.

"Save your breath, baby, focus on your healing," Ambrose shushed Kyree, his voice trembling.

"D-Dog..." Kyree repeated, trying to lace some urgency into his voice, "dog..."

"Ambrose, how long does healing take? He doesn't seem to be getting any better," Saige sounded terrified, holding Kyree's hand so tight he was surprised his bones hadn't broken.

"It should be instant- it should-" Ambrose stopped abruptly, lifting the hand that wasn't holding Kyree's wound shut to his mouth and licking a drop of blood from his finger. Kyree couldn't quite make out the noise Ambrose made. Like a curt, pained whine, or maybe a whimper of frustration. Either way, it didn't sound good.

"It's devil's snare, it's stopping him from healing," Ambrose sounded distraught, "Saige, I-I don't know what to do - he's losing too much blood - he can't - I don't -" it was then that Kyree heard a soft sob from Ambrose, "I don't know what to do," he admitted, his voice so weak, so quiet, so vulnerable. Kyree knew the feeling, knew the feeling too damn well. He tried to tell Ambrose how much he loved him, tried to tell him he would get past his death, would learn to love another as he had. But his mouth wouldn't move, no part of his body would listen to his brain despite it screaming and yelling to fight.

"Abigor," Saige said suddenly, hope in her tone, "Ambrose, summon Abigor. Do it now, maybe he can take it. Maybe his healing is stronger. Ambrose, this is your only chance, do it," Saige insisted, restoring some sense of faith to Ambrose. Ambrose and Kyree were bathed in an amber glow as Ambrose focused with every fibre in his being. Saige had to look away when the light got to a blinding peak, but instantly snapped her gaze back when it dwindled.

In her arms was Abigor, an expression of deep agony across his face. His horns were somehow even longer, with those same silver flecks as Ambrose's. He had silver around his obsidian eyes too, as if it lined them and faded into his tanned skin as it spread.

"He's fading," Abigor forced out, his already gruff voice somehow rougher with each word, feeling Kyree's grip on reality slipping. Saige gave a half sob, turning to the crowd as they gaped at the new being before them.

"Lucifer!" she screamed, tears still flowing down her cheeks at a steady pace, "Lucifer!" she had no idea where her grandfather was. Or where any of Kyree's family was. As though they had just vanished.

"I've got him," Lucifer reassured Saige when he appeared on the other side of Abigor's body, slipping his hand under his back and feeling for the wound, "he's healing, slowly, but he's healing," Saige let out a sigh of relief, which mixed with another panicked sob. Abigor's lips curved into half smile as he gazed on at Saige.

"This is why you are their favourite daughter," Abigor sounded strained, stained and weary.

"I'm their only daughter," Saige responded with a weak laugh, brushing back a few strands of Abigor's brunette hair from his face. Abigor's mouth twitched a little as though he wanted to speak again, but he didn't have the strength. Saige glanced at Lucifer fearfully, not wanting Abigor to close his eyes.

"Let him rest, he is healing. They will be OK, Saige, thanks to you," Abigor's eyes finally fluttered closed, as the tranquillity of unconsciousness lulled him and his Master's into, sadly, a darkened dream from Kyree's mind...

"Where is he? He's late," Kyree pushed through the thick crowd of people, scanning every face in search of his lover. He wasn't there. He was almost 20 minutes late and guests were getting restless.

"Father!" Kyree called out as he saw Orion stood with his mother, "father, have you seen him?" panic was rising in Kyree, his heart almost beating out of his chest, sorrow building within him.

"No, son, I'm so sorry," Orion patted his son's shoulder, a gesture that was all he could really do at that time. His mother had a much more sympathetic look on her face, a soft frown of pain knotting her brows.

"Oh, Ky, you didn't deserve this. I thought he truly loved you," Yennifer cupped her child's cheeks, hoping her affection could make up some small part of what he lost with his lover.

"He does love me, mother, have some faith," Kyree snapped, stepping back out of his mother's reach, sick of everyone thinking his lover had left him, "I have to find him, he must have lost track of time," Kyree sped off again, shouldering through the guests who had exited their seats as their patience ran dry, ignoring their tutting and complaining about his rudeness.

"Idella!" Kyree's brother was leaning against the stone wall of the church, his eyes on the ground, "Idella, brother, please tell me you've seen him," Idella had a look of guilt on his face too, but who didn't by that time.

"He went to the human world, Ky. He didn't say-" Kyree had disappeared before he had chance to hear the rest, appearing in a small, quaint apartment.

"Lex?!" Kyree called out, his eyes scanning the apartment for any sign of his fiance, "Lex, I know you're here!" Kyree sighed deeply when Alexander stepped out from a room opposite him, "you're late for our fucking wedding, Lex, what the fuck is wrong with you?" Kyree seethed, detesting how calm Alexander looked as he leant against the door frame.

"Can you keep your voice down, Kyree? I have a splitting headache and I don't really want Maxwell waking up," the relaxed tone in Alexander's voice grated on Kyree's nerves, making his anger flare up within him.

"Alexander, it is our wedding day," Kyree said each word slowly, with such definition he was sure Alexander would show some sort of emotion.

"Thank you for stating the obvious, Kyree, for the second time. Do you need the ring back now or should I mail it to you?" Kyree lost it then, stalked over to Alexander, slamming him against the wall, hoping it would knock some sense into him. Alexander merely chuckled, a glint of mischief in his green eyes, a glint of lust.

"Oh, you always were one who liked to get rough, bunny," Kyree's hands were clutching tight onto Alexander's shirt, that was until Alexander moved his left hand to his throat, "come on, bunny, you know I like it like that. Do it, I know you want to, I know you're just desperate to give a little squeeze because of what I did today," Alexander sounded just a little breathless, despite Kyree vowing to himself to apply no pressure to his throat, no matter how much he taunted him. Alexander rolled his hips forward, brushing his body against Kyree's, flaunting his arousal at the whole situation. Kyree simply clenched his jaw and made a move to step back.

"Don't you dare," Alexander hissed, tightening his grip on Kyree's arms, holding him in place, "I didn't say you could let go."

"Alexander, let-" Kyree's speech ceased when Alexander's palm struck his cheek, considerably more gentle than the usual force Kyree was subjected to. Kyree's eyes darkened and he couldn't help tightening his fingers around his fiance's throat. Alexander choked out a strangled laugh, goading Kyree to do more, hurt him more.

"No, Alexander, this is wrong," Kyree made another attempt to move away from Alexander but his fiance again just wouldn't let him go.

"You're fucking pathetic, Kyree, " Alexander seethed, his demeanour suddenly growing so much darker, "you can't do anything right. You don't even know how to be angry at me for God sake. Fucking pathetic. And you wonder why I don't want to marry you, maybe it's because that man sleeping in the room behind you is so much better than you.

"He treats me better than you, loves me better than you, even fucks me better than you. You will never find anyone else to love you, Kyree, because you can't be loved. I'm your one and only chance at companionship so you better fucking grovel at my feet if you don't want me to leave you," Kyree saw red then. He ignored all warning from the better part of his mind to just walk away and instead tightened his hand so much around Alexander's throat that he saw bruises visibly forming under his fingers.

Alexander struggled for only a few seconds before his eyes rolled back in his head and his body went limp under Kyree's grasp. Realising what he had done, Kyree let go of Alexander, tears forming in his eyes as his fiance's body tumbled to the ground.

"Lex?" he whispered, unable to quell the flood of tears that began to stream down his cheeks, "Lex, wake up, I'm sorry," Kyree sobbed as he knelt next to his lover, cradling the corpse in his arms, hoping Alexander was just playing another cruel trick on him.

But he wasn't. Alexander was dead. Kyree had killed him. And now he was truly alone...

Chapter 26

Kyree couldn't deny the ache that spread through him as he crawled his way to consciousness. With each step closer to the light, another stab of pain shot through him, urging him to scuttle back into the darkness and remain there. Part of him wanted to. A large part. The darkness seemed comforting, the gelid tendrils of shadow reaching out to soothe him.

The light was sharp, sharp and bright. It hurt, burning him as he neared it, searing his flesh and sending smouldering ash through his lungs. Light meant good, or was supposed to mean that anyway. It was always associated with happiness and contentment, not sorrow and grief. Maybe the light had just gone out in Kyree's life, maybe that was why his light caused so much suffering.

Kyree wasn't sure how long his inner turmoil had gone on, but when he awoke it was no longer night. He was laid on a bed, the bed he shared with Ambrose, in the room he shared with Ambrose. Somehow, the thought of Ambrose no longer filled him with elation, instead simply elicited a dull sense of torment.

Kyree was alone in the room, he was thankful for that in some aspects. There was barely any pain in his back, which he was not thankful for. He yearned for pain, yearned to feel something, anything. He deserved the pain, deserved every aching minute of it.

As he entered the en-suite bathroom, he surveyed his dishevelled appearance in the pristine mirror. His hair was matted with blood, in fact, his entire face and chest had blood spatter across it. He was only wearing the slacks from the coronation, his torso completely bare.

His eyes looked dull. The colour was barely there but they weren't black, no, almost grey. He looked tired, he looked God damn exhausted. They were bloodshot too, as though he had been crying. He wondered if he had, if whilst that awful memory played on loop he had truly been crying.

The sight of his own face disgusted him. It was the last thing Alexander had seen before he had murdered him. Murdered. That was the word. The word no one liked, the word Kyree would be haunted by for the rest of his life.

Kyree didn't even realise what he had done until the sound of glass shattering roused him from his thoughts. He focused on his image in the mirror once again, seeing a distorted and mutilated version through the shards of glass still held there. His gaze flittered down to his bloodied fist, pieces of glass stuck out awkwardly in the skin between the knuckles.

He broke then, stumbling back until he hit the cold tiles of the wall behind him, sobbing softly. His body slid down the wall as he curled his knees up to his chest, his body shaking with the force of his weeping. He wasn't sure how long he stayed like that, time didn't really feel the same anymore, nothing felt the same.

He didn't look up until two arms wrapped around him, pulling him into a warm, familiar chest. Ambrose. Kyree clutched his lover's shirt as he sobbed, never wanting to let go, never wanting Ambrose to leave.

"It's OK, Ky, I got you, you're OK," Ambrose held onto Kyree's trembling form, tears in his own eyes at the extent of Kyree's pain. He could feel it. He truly could feel the darkness spreading through Kyree. He wouldn't burden him with that fact, didn't want him to know how he had felt every emotion from Kyree since the brand had appeared on their arms.

A tear trickled from Ambrose's eye, a single one that he didn't quite manage to hold onto. But it was just the beginning. As he allowed the floodgates to open, allowed himself to cry with Kyree, for Kyree, he bit down on his lip, not wanting to make a sound. He wasn't sure Kyree could bounce back from what he had experienced. And that terrified him.

In the coming days, it was Saige that first noticed it. Kyree was irritable, quick to snap at the little things, distant. It's like he's cutting ties, she had said when she mentioned this to Ambrose, like he's getting ready to die. Ambrose had muttered some half-assed response that Kyree would never do that, that he was a fighter and he wouldn't just give up.

Ambrose held onto that thought for the next week, held on tight as if it was the only thing keeping him sane. But he noticed changes too. Kyree barely looked at him, shied away from his touch, even insisted on sleeping in different beds. He was so afraid of hurting Ambrose physically that he didn't see the emotional damage he was causing.

Still, Ambrose denied Kyree's worsening condition. Until that day. That day he found him in the bathroom with a rope. He was simply staring at it in his hands, staring at the noose he had made, at the slip knot. Ambrose knew then that Kyree was not going to just get better by himself and with willpower alone. He needed help.

Kyree shrugged off the arm Ambrose wrapped around him the second their skin touched, taking a side step to the left to force distance between them. Ambrose sighed, slipping his hand into Kyree's and flashing a soft glare in his direction when he felt him trying to tug his hand away.

The door in front of the two swung open, revealing a man with a half smile holding a little girl on his hip. She was babbling, a toy horse in one hand and a Barbie in the other. Adorable was the first word that came to mind for Ambrose, who suddenly wished he could have seen Saige growing up.

"I was just wondering where the two of you were, Zepp thought you might not be coming," Ambrose returned the smile as Maxwell stepped to the side, allowing him to partially drag Kyree into the apartment.

Maxwell Hurse was not a difficult man to find. He was very prominent on social media, Facebook being a particular favourite of his, and ran a small catering business out of his apartment that he shared with his husband and daughter. The same apartment he had not moved out of after the death of his boyfriend almost five years ago.

"Wouldn't miss this for the world," Ambrose turned his attention to the little girl who was staring at both Kyree and him, "and who is this little beauty?" Maxwell grinned proudly, bouncing the little girl gently.

"This is Teddy. Teddy, can you say hi to Ambrose and Kyree?" Maxwell cooed, glancing at Kyree in the hopes that his daughter would have brought some happiness to him. But Kyree wasn't even looking at Teddy, his eyes instead fixed on the floor next to the doorway to Maxwell's bedroom.

"Her name is Bella," Maxwell caught the tail end of his daughter's babbling, surprised at how interested Ambrose actually looked as she told him all about her dolls.

"Zepp, can you watch Teddy for a while? Ambrose and Kyree are here," Maxwell called toward the kitchen. Another man darted out, flour down his clothing and his hair looking particularly out of place.

"Cookies, my dear Teddy, I need your fairy magic to help make them or they just won't cook and where would we be then?" the man announced, placing a soft kiss on Maxwell's stubbled cheek and holding out his arms for Teddy.

"Can Bella and Hailee help, daddy?" Teddy asked with a giggle.

"I wouldn't have it any other way, baby," Teddy wrapped her arms around Zepp as he lifted her from Maxwell, "would either of you like a drink? Coffee? Tea? Tequila?" Ambrose chuckled but Kyree remained completely silent.

"He's joking about the tequila," Maxwell muttered, instructing Zepp to return to the kitchen and be quiet, feigning anger. But Ambrose did catch the soft chuckle as Teddy asked if she could have some tequila.

"Please, sit," Maxwell motioned toward the two opposing couches with a coffee table in the middle. Ambrose glanced toward Kyree, startled by the haunted expression on his face as a tear trickled down his pale cheek. He was still staring at that damn corner.

"Oh, baby," Ambrose instinctively stepped closer, reaching up to touch Kyree's cheek but his expression only worsened. Ambrose bit down on his lip, dropping his hand to his side, not sure what he could do to help his struggling lover.

"May I?" Maxwell asked softly, gingerly brushing his fingertips across Ambrose's shoulder as he passed him, "Kyree? Kyree, can you look at me please?" his voice was very gentle, very soothing as he spoke to Kyree, "I need you to look at me, Kyree," it took a few seconds, but Kyree's gaze finally met Maxwell's, "my God, it truly is killing you, isn't it? Kyree, you need to calm down, OK? Letting this consume you isn't going to help anyone, least of all yourself. Come sit down and talk to me," somehow, Maxwell got Kyree to sit on the couch with him. Ambrose opted to sit on the one opposite them, not wanting his presence to distress Kyree anymore than it already was.

"Alexander was not a good man, Kyree. You have to remember that. He was abusive, manipulative and vindictive. He is not worth the pain you are putting yourself through," Maxwell clasped Kyree's hands, seeing them visibly trembling as the demon attempted to hold himself together, "if you hadn't have done what you did that day, someone else would have no doubt. You saved us both that day. Had Alexander still been alive today, where would we be?

"I would still be a drugged up junkie with no livelihood, that is if I hadn't died already. And you, you would still be caught up in his web of control. You would have never met Ambrose and you would not have a daughter. I would have never met Zeppelin and I wouldn't have Teddy. We're better off without him, I assure you," Kyree's tears had not stopped, but they definitely slowed the more Maxwell spoke, "Ambrose told me about the other day, when he found you with the rope. I want you to tell me what you were thinking, what you were feeling, in that moment," a twinge of pain shot through Ambrose's heart, he did not want to hear Kyree talk about his thoughts at his lowest point.

"I hated myself," Kyree began, his voice broken and raspy from crying, "I still do. I didn't feel anything and that was the point. I was numb. I didn't see a point in living anymore. Being tormented by the image of my hands around his throat every day, it was torture.

"But it was got worse. His face started to become Ambrose's," Ambrose's breath hitched in his throat, his chest tightening, "or sometimes it would be Saige's. I just couldn't live with myself knowing I was capable of something like that. Killing myself seemed like the only option to keep everyone else safe-" Kyree stopped as Ambrose rose to his feet, exiting the room with his hand covering his mouth, trying to reduce the sound of his sobbing.

"I know you can hear him, Kyree," Maxwell said softly, "listen to him now, listen to what you are doing to him. Forget what you're feeling and what you're thinking, listen to what your self-hate is doing to those you love."

Ambrose wasn't really sure where he was going but somehow ended up in the kitchen when searching for somewhere to be alone. Zeppelin immediately guided him to a chair, placing a glass of water in front of him and sitting opposite. Ambrose stared at his hands, listening to the soft patter of his tears hitting the table.

"He won't even let me touch him, y'know," Ambrose murmured between silent sobs, "I can't even hold him when he's crying, or when he's trying to hurt himself. It just makes him worse. Y'know what that's like? Not being able to do anything for the person you love when they're at their worst. It's like someone tearing your heart from your chest and just ripping it apart piece by piece. I don't know how much longer I can stay," Kyree felt like he'd been stabbed all over again when he heard those 9 muffled words, "I love him, with all my heart. I mean, I would do anything for him. I would take this pain from him if I could, I would do it in a heartbeat. But I don't know if I can wait around and watch him die. It's no longer a question of what if I find him dead. It's when."

Chapter 27

- -

Nothing seemed to have changed after their visit to Maxwell and Zeppelin. Kyree was still the same. Maybe even a little worse. Maxwell had told Ambrose to give him a little time by himself to come to terms with his loss, Ambrose opted to give him a week.

5 days into that week, something changed in Kyree. Like a switch flipped in his mind. The haze of grief and self-pity seemed to lift, taking with it the fatigue and heartache. He felt alive again, he just felt everything again. He decided to go on a run, having been cooped up inside for God knows how long.

Endwin joined him, despite his injuries from the assassin. Kyree did wonder what Endwin had inflicted upon his attacker, much worse than what he had gotten. Kyree kept his pace slow, so Endwin could keep up with him, but soon his dog was outrunning him by quite a while.

As he tried to catch up, he allowed a small smile to curve up the corners of his mouth. He enjoyed the feeling of wind rushing around him, the sound of his feet hitting the floor, his breath coming out in short, sharp bursts. He made a promise to himself as he stopped to catch his breath that he was going to get Saige and Ambrose to come on a run with him next time.

Kyree chuckled to himself when he noticed how long he had been out, deciding an hour was probably long enough to have run off the residual depression. His stomach agreed, making an awfully loud noise. He had barely eaten for almost 3 weeks, maybe he could badger Ambrose into cooking something for him. The thought of Ambrose awoke a different type of hunger within him, God he missed him.

It took him a further half an hour to find his way back to the royal palace through the thick forest that surrounded it. He could have just appeared back in their bedroom but he truly enjoyed being outside.

Endwin seemed altogether exhausted as they entered the palace, almost collapsing by the door. Kyree smiled softly at his pet, filling a bowl with water and stooping down to ruffle the fur on his head.

"Never got a chance to thank you, End, you saved my life," he murmured happily. Endwin, whether he understood what Kyree was saying or not, simply made a content little whine, lapping up some of the water before laying back and drifting to sleep.

Ambrose hadn't been in their bedroom, he never really had been since Kyree had gotten seriously bad. So Kyree assumed he was probably in his office, and his assumption was correct. Kyree simply stood and stared at Ambrose through the half-open door, knowing Ambrose had yet to notice him.

Ambrose was wearing a suit, as usual, that man never did understand the concept of casual clothing. But the blazer was hung around the back of his chair, and the sleeves of pristine white shirt were rolled up to his elbows. The brand was on display, Kyree wondered if Abigor got restless when he wasn't called upon for so long. Maybe they would let him out for a run later.

Despite the deep purple bags under his eyes, Ambrose looked the same gorgeous man Kyree always saw. His brows were knotted together into a soft frown as he kept his gaze on his laptop, only adding to his bewitching appearance. When the time came that Kyree was no longer content with simply observing Ambrose, he strolled into the room, closing the door behind him.

Ambrose glanced up, looking a little sheepish. Kyree was shirtless, wearing only a pair of tight black sweatpants that hugged every inch of him, leaving not much to the imagination as they hung low on his hips. Ambrose's lips twitched, and Kyree wished he would allow that wicked little smirk to consume him, but his mouth remained set in a hard line.

"How are you feeling?" Ambrose asked gently, his voice soft as he spoke. Kyree wasn't surprised at this, though he missed Ambrose's confidence, he knew this would be the case for a short while until Ambrose truly realised Kyree was better.

"Honestly?" Kyree strode over to Ambrose's desk, standing opposite and resting his hands on the smooth wood, "horny as fuck," Kyree ran his tongue over his bottom lip, gauging Ambrose's reaction. He still looked sceptical, not truly believing Kyree was back to his same flirty self. With a soft chuckle, Kyree moved around the table, tugging back Ambrose's chair and straddling his lap. Ambrose had a hell of a lot of restraint to keep his arms by his side as Kyree leant forward, catching his earlobe between his teeth and rolling his tongue over it gently.

"Touch me, babe," Kyree purred, his teeth grazing against Ambrose's stubbled jawline as he moved his mouth toward his lover's, "c'mon, I know you want to, I can feel how much you want to," Kyree pressed his hips down ever so slightly, eliciting a sharp gasp from Ambrose, yet still he felt no hands on him, "do I have to do all the work?" Kyree's lips neared Ambrose's, but he pulled them back a little as they barely brushed against his lover's. Ambrose's eyes had darkened, the colour lost beneath their obsidian finish, they were wide too, a little fear in them. Kyree shook his head, his smirk widening.

"Would you like me to beg?" Kyree bit down tenderly on Ambrose's bottom lip and that seemed to be all he needed to show his lover he truly wanted him. Ambrose's left hand pushed Kyree's head closer as their mouths collided, his other hand tightening around Kyree's waist, holding him still. He tugged on Kyree's hair, coaxing a soft gasp from him and taking full advantage of his open mouth.

"Are you sure?" Ambrose broke the kiss for just a second, but Kyree simply reconnected their lips in response. Kyree's hands fumbled down the buttons of Ambrose's shirt, craving the feeling of his lover's skin on his. He splayed his hands out over Ambrose's bare torso, feeling every bump and ridge of his well-defined muscles.

"Strip," Ambrose growled, his voice lower than Kyree had ever heard, "now," slipping off Ambrose's lap, Kyree took his time removing the sweatpants, revelling in the lustrous, half-lidded stare Ambrose supplied him with. When Kyree was done with his little show, Ambrose rose to his feet, letting his open shirt fall from his shoulders in the process. Ambrose took a hold of Kyree's elbow, spinning him around and bending him over the desk.

"Stay," he commanded, running his index finger down the curvature of Kyree's spine. Kyree let out a soft whimper as he felt the piercing sting of Ambrose's hand across his bare ass. It would leave a mark, there was no doubt of that, yet that just turned Kyree on even more. The familiar jingling of Ambrose's belt unbuckling filled Kyree with anticipation, and even a little fear.

Ambrose didn't give any sort of warning, simply buried himself completely in Kyree with one movement. A groan left Ambrose as a small cry of pain slipped from Kyree. Tears sprung to Kyree's eyes, the sharp aching throb he had missed so much returning, he would have to get accustomed to this kind of rough love all over again.

Ambrose leant over, hastily trailing a line along the soft skin of Kyree's throat with his lips, catching the flesh between his teeth every so often to ensure a mark would remain. His pace was fast, and soon the pleasure outweighed the pain for Kyree.

Moans of varying length and volume escaped the two men, mingling with the creaking of the desk and the sounds of skin hitting skin. Kyree moaned some warped version of Ambrose's name as he tipped over into ecstasy, his lover following not too long after. Words couldn't describe the feeling, the intimacy, the pleasure, all rolled into one was so... intense.

Somehow, in the hazy aftermath, Kyree found himself curled up on Ambrose's lap with his lover's shirt loosely around him. Kyree's arms were wrapped around Ambrose's neck, his head rested on his chest and his legs dangling either side of his lover's lap. It felt wonderful to be held again.

Ambrose set his chin upon Kyree's head, contemplating whatever had happened in the past half an hour with a sated smile on his face. Eventually, he had to get back to his work, but didn't mind having to do so around his slumbering lover. He could see Kyree's dream playing in the back of his mind, it was a pleasant one, that Ambrose happily focused in on every so often.

He was just finishing writing up an email when there was a soft knock on his door. He glanced down at Kyree, thankful that the desk covered both Kyree's ass and his lower body entirely. He was shirtless, but that truly didn't bother him.

"Come in," he kept his voice low, ensuring he wouldn't wake Kyree. Saige entered, a startled expression on her face as her eyes landed on Kyree.

"Oh, I assumed you would be alone, am I interrupting something?" she asked nervously, unsure whether she truly wanted to know the answer.

"Had you walked in 15 minutes earlier, my dear, you would have learnt the ins and outs of gay sex first hand," Kyree mumbled sleepily into Ambrose's chest, not bothering to open his eyes. Ambrose hadn't even noticed that Kyree had awoken.

"Kyree," Ambrose scolded, trying, and failing, to suppress a small bout of laughter, "not in front of our daughter please," Kyree made a low sound of appreciation as Ambrose rubbed small circles in the base of his back, kneading the flesh back to life.

"How are you, dad?" Saige walked closer to the desk, perching on the chair that stood the other side.

"Back and better than ever," Kyree turned his head slightly to glance at his daughter. She looked paler than usual, but overall there wasn't much change from when Kyree had last taken the time to truly appreciate her appearance.

"When did this happen?"

"Mmm... about three hours ago. Just woke up and felt..." Kyree paused, trying to think of a word to describe how he had felt when he had awoken, "everything. Felt normal again, just like that. Begs the question, don't you think? Was all that morbid depression truly from me?" Saige had that same little frown Ambrose had when she was thinking about something in depth, it put a smile on Kyree's face each and every time.

"What do you mean?"

"You think it was something else that caused you to feel that way?" Ambrose chimed in, his frown mirroring Saige's.

"It's possible, don't you think? I mean, it all feels like the past three weeks was just one long dream. I've never had suicidal contemplation before, ever, even after Alexander's death, I never thought about killing myself. I mean, the night I found out what I had done to Alexander, sure it affected me deeply, but not enough to make me truly want to kill myself.

"The last thing I would want to do would be leave the people I love feeling the exact same way I had felt after losing Alexander. I would never do that to you, to either of you. And if I died," Kyree turned his attention to Ambrose, caressing his thumb up over his smooth cheek, "you wouldn't just lose me, you'd lose Saige too and I couldn't ever do that to you," Ambrose smiled warmly, kissing the underside of Kyree's palm and wrist as it neared his lips.

"What do you mean he would lose me too?" Saige interrupted, sounding a little more nervous than before.

"We don't usually tell our children this, my dear, but if a sire dies, everyone they have turned dies too. If I had killed myself, my blood tie to you would be cut off and you would simply die, return to being merely a corpse," Saige's eyes widened slightly, her lips parted in a silent gasp.

"So if you had been killed at your trial?"

"You would have died too, yes, my dear," Ambrose explained, "I didn't want to burden you with that additional fear after what you were already going through," not wanting to indulge anything more fearful to Saige, Ambrose changed the subject, "I'll ask my father if he's heard of anything. Now, baby, you need to go get dressed, we're having lunch with everyone, I have an announcement."

Chapter 28

Whatever Ambrose's announcement was, he had been keeping under wraps since before he had been coronated. Kyree couldn't get Saige to divulge even the slightest detail of what it was, no matter how much he badgered or bribed her.

"I can tie my own tie, Ambrose," Kyree huffed for the third time, with a playful roll of his eyes.

"Stop complaining, you love the attention," Ambrose retorted, kissing Kyree's nose as he straightened the deep blue tie.

"We're having lunch, not getting married, Ambrose, must we dress up?" Kyree took hold of Ambrose's hands, "how about we just skip lunch? We could get undressed and have a little time alone? Make up for the last three weeks all in one afternoon?" Ambrose chuckled softly, kissing the knuckles on Kyree's hands in turn.

"That would be your cock talking, baby, not your brain. We are not skipping lunch," Kyree pouted, even contemplated whining, but when Ambrose made up his mind there was no changing it for anything.

Kyree allowed Ambrose to lead him, hand in hand, toward the large dining room that he did not have many great memories in. Kyree had not entered the room many times, and in those times he had queried multiples times why a family with three people needed such a large room to eat three meals in.

The first time he had seen the room, he had been in awe at the beauty of the decor. Ambrose had informed him that it was his great-grandfather who had built the palace and his grandfather had been the one to refurbish it with most of the items that were still there to that day.

Of course, the first time he had entered the room was also when Abigor had nearly choked Essence to death so Kyree didn't really cherish the memory. In the room this time, there were many more people than Kyree expected to see for "just lunch" as Ambrose had called it.

"Kyree, my baby," Yennifer cooed, dashing over to dote all over Kyree as soon as she set eyes on him, "oh, how are you, honey?" Kyree loved his mother dearly but by God she was irritating. She constantly babied him, despite his age being closer to a millennium than a hundred, and it was just getting plain embarrassing.

"Yen, give him some space, he's not five, my dear," Orion chided his wife, tugging her hands gently from Kyree's cheeks.

"Oh, Ori, but I haven't seen him in so long and-"

"I'm fine, mother, really," Kyree interjected, kissing his mother on the cheek, "Ambrose is taking good care of me," Kyree flashed a sly smile toward Ambrose and was tugged closer by the elder demon.

"I pity the poor bastard," Idella chimed in, a smug expression on his face as he patted his brother's shoulder, "glad you're back to somewhat normality, brother."

"Empathetic as ever, baby brother, I wouldn't expect any more," just as Kyree was about to pull his brother into a hug, he noticed Saige stood, talking with Lucifer, draped against the arm of Tyrell. The mere sight of the demon caused Kyree's blood to boil and the colour to drain from his beautiful eyes.

"What is he doing here?" Kyree seethed, unable to remove his eyes from the invading specimen in the room. Ambrose caressed the back of Kyree's hand, excusing them from speaking with his parents and leading him closer to Tyrell.

"Saige invited him, baby, and I think we give him one final chance," Kyree glowered at Ambrose, his lover clearly did not understand the deep disdain, "come on, Ky, you don't even have to talk to him face to face, OK? Just ignore him," just ignore him? Easier said than done when the distance between the two opposing forces was being reduced and Kyree's anger was still building ever higher.

"Kyree," Lucifer, despite no longer being the king, still acted like one. His presence was always felt and his voice reverberated throughout any room he was ever in. Kyree attempted a smile, but could feel the smug stare of Tyrell burning down the back of his neck.

"How are you?" that question was going to get old fast, Kyree thought to himself, thankful his bond with Ambrose didn't give them any sort of telepathic gifts. He was sure no one would want to look into his mind for the next hour or so.

"Better, thank you."

"Actually, speaking of Kyree's recovery," Ambrose lowered his voice, not wanting all in the room to hear his conversation with his father, "have you ever heard of any sort of substance that could cause such emotional distortion as Kyree experienced?" Lucifer instantly looked grim, a deep sigh wracking his body.

"It is rare, but yes, I have heard of such a plant that can do that. It is known as blood root. It is a form of devil's snare that only grows in the arid plains of the human world, very difficult to grow and even more so to harvest. It heightens whatever emotion is being felt in that moment, to a point of self-annihilation.

"It has to enter the bloodstream, so in a sense is a venom, not a poison, but only a drop is needed. It takes time to incubate, maybe a week before the effects are truly fatal. I imagine the assassin probably mixed it in with the devil's snare on the knife so it was not detected.

"It has no scent, no discernable flavour either, simply a blood red colour, hence the name. In Kyree's case, he experienced heightened grief, which is probably exactly what the assassin wanted. It works with most emotions; happiness, envy, sadness, lust. Anything," Ambrose shared a pained glance with Kyree, both reminiscing the lowest point Kyree got to in the previous weeks.

"So, he's given up trying to kill us, he wants to drive us to doing it ourselves. Wonderful," Kyree muttered sarcastically with a roll of his still darkened eyes.

"How can you live like this?" Saige interjected, her watery eyes set in a frown, "constantly dodging attempts on your life, never able to just relax. For lack of a better word, it's hell," Kyree watched as Tyrell pulled Saige into his chest, murmuring something into her lilac hair. A gesture as simple as that, benign as it is, awoke the urge within Kyree to rip him limb from limb.

As everyone sat down to lunch, Kyree tried his best to refrain from growling at the sight of Tyrell speaking so freely and calmly with his family. That man would not grow on him. Kyree would wait for just one simple slip up, just one was all he needed to justify filleting pieces of skin from the demon's body.

Midway through the meal, as the conversation seemed to die down, all attention turned to Ambrose and Kyree sat at the head of the table. Kyree remained silent, not in the mood yet to attempt small talk, he had always detested that aspect of social interaction. Kyree was about to make some half-assed comment when Ambrose chose to speak instead.

"Kyree went through a rough patch in the past few weeks, which we're still trying to figure out. But, seeing him the way he was, it made me realise something," Ambrose rose from his chair, withdrawing something from his pocket, sending just a small spike of apprehension through Kyree, "I have never loved a man more than I love Kyree, never felt so alive with someone," Ambrose dropped to one knee and Kyree's eyes widened as he opened a small velvet box. Nestled in the middle of that box was a ring. The band was a glistening white gold with cobalt blue gems inlaid into the metal. Kyree knew exactly what it was based off, the fish in his dream.

"I don't ever want you to go through what you went through recently again, but if you do, I want you to go through it knowing you're my husband. I want you to know that I will forever be there for you, to support you, to love you, even to cry with you. I will be there. Kyree Landon, will you marry me?" Kyree shook his head gently, a grin on his face but tears in his eyes.

"Of course," Kyree leant forward, pressing a passionate kiss to Ambrose's lips, smiling into the gesture as he felt Ambrose slip the ring on his finger. The room erupted with applause and cheering which died down pretty damn quick when a small black box appeared in Kyree's hand.

"Well, I guess that makes my plans for tonight redundant, I might as well give you this now," Kyree opened the little box, revealing a silver ring with a swirled obsidian inlay, "my grandfather's ring, that I was going to propose to you with later this evening. Which I did tell our daughter earlier this morning," all eyes turned to Saige, who smiled innocently.

"Saige Landon-" Ambrose began but was quickly cut off by Saige.

"It's Saige Ross now, I mean, I assumed Kyree will be taking your name, what with it being a royal bloodline," she giggled, standing from her chair and walking over to embrace her father's, "and what was I supposed to do? Tell Kyree not to propose because you were going to? Or tell you not to propose because Kyree was going to? I wanted it to be a surprise so I figured whoever asks first gets the pleasure of doing so," Kyree chuckled, kissing the top of Saige's hair. Ambrose smiled as Kyree slipped the ring on his finger and they shared in another, slightly shorter kiss. As everyone sat back down, returning to their conversations, Kyree moved closer to Ambrose, each exchanging vows of eternal love in hushed voices before sealing their affection with one last kiss.

Chapter 29

Saige ventured back to her bedroom, adorning a beaming grin, after listening to her father's proposals. Her love for them was growing to an insurmountable level and she wondered if anything else would ever be able to top her two bewitching demon fathers.

"Mmm, that dress," Tyrell rumbled huskily, his gaze locked on the tight powder blue fabric hugging Saige's petite body, specifically her gorgeous ass. Saige giggled, turning as she reached her bedroom and pulling Tyrell in to kiss her, their bodies colliding together as they stumbled through the doorway.

Tyrell's hand slid down her body to bunch up the dress, in the hopes that she would finally let him peel it off her. Saige batted his hands away with each attempt, but not with any particular amount of force, nothing that would stop him from trying again and again.

"Stop, Ty," she breathed, adding just a slight more force to her movements, "Ty," pressing her hands on Tyrell's chest, thrusting the elder demon away from her to grasp some sort of sense of control over herself.

"Saige, I'm sorry," Tyrell ran his thumb down Saige's pale left cheek, pressing a chaste kiss to her forehead. Saige knew Tyrell did that too often to truly forgive. He was constantly throwing himself at her and she happened to wonder if he wanted her simply to flaunt it in Kyree's face, he was shallow enough for that.

But she didn't want to believe her first boyfriend since she had turned was merely with her to piss off her father. So she forgave him time and time again, absently believing he had just lost control for a few moments, despite knowing deeper down that that wasn't the case.

"Will you come to my father's wedding with me?" Saige asked sheepishly, her lips brushing tenderly against Tyrell's chest.

"Of course, beautiful, I would love to," Tyrell placed another kiss on Saige's head, this time on top of her mane of lilac hair, "what happened to him was so awful. It's such a shame his parents had to leave early to take Idella home because he was taken ill, maybe if they had been there he would not have had such severe injuries," at the mention of Idella's sickness, Saige's expression dropped. She looked startled as she backed away from Tyrell, maybe even bordering on terror.

"It... it was you," she breathed, her body beginning to tremble, "y-you poisoned him, y-you got Idella sick so Yennifer and Orion would take him home," Tyrell reached out to touch Saige's arms, to hold her still so he could explain himself, but she ducked away from his touch, "Kyr-" Saige's cries were cut off by Tyrell clamping his hand over her mouth, simply adding to the fear she already felt.

"Must you be so loud, my sweet?" Tyrell growled, using his free hand to catch both of Saige's wrists between his fingers, stilling her body as she whimpered softly, "I didn't want to get you involved, beautiful, I was hoping to keep you. You would make a pretty little pet," Tyrell shifted the hand inhibiting Saige's speech to cover her nose as well, cutting off her supply of oxygen. Her tears ceased then, her struggling increasing in force as panic swelled within her. She was going to die. Tyrell was going to kill her solely to keep her quiet.

As the oxygen within her dwindled, so did Saige's strength. Her vision seemed to be darkening, the awful burning sensation in her chest seeping into a cold numbness. One final tear trickled down Saige's pale cheek, her body losing all stability and simply collapsing against Tyrell, the darkness of unconsciousness seeming much more appealing...

Then suddenly the hand around Saige's mouth and nose was wrenched away and she was falling forward. She pushed her arms out in front of her just in time to stop her head hitting the wooden flooring, coughing and gasping for much-needed air. When she composed herself, holding her aching wrist that had hit the floor at an odd angle, she saw none other than Abigor.

The enormous creature was throwing Tyrell around the room as though he was simply a ragdoll. In the seconds Saige had been focusing on staying conscious, Abigor seemed to have already broken Tyrell's left arm, jaw and probably quite a few ribs. As much as Saige wanted to allow Abigor to rip Tyrell to pieces, she knew he had helped the assassin, therefore may know his identity.

"Wait..." she wheezed, her throat throbbing with each breath she forced down, "stop..." Saige tried to push herself up onto her elbows but hadn't the strength. She was about to roll over and simply allow her body to fall into the welcoming abyss when she felt a pair of hands helping her to a sitting position.

"Hey, you're OK, sweetheart, you're safe," Ambrose's soothing voice lulled the fear out of Saige as she relaxed against his chest, taking slow, shallow breaths as he instructed.

"He knows the assassin," she whispered weakly, watching as Kyree's fist came into contact with Tyrell's bloodied face again, "he's the one who poisoned Idella," Saige wasn't sure if Ambrose had even heard her, she was barely audible to her own ears, let alone someone else's.

"Ky, stop," judging by Ambrose's frown, Saige assumed Kyree wasn't listening to his fiance, "Kyree, stop!" Ambrose's booming voice echoed throughout the room, making Saige flinch with the sudden volume change, "he is working with the assassin, leave Osiris and Anubis to get any information out of him, no more blood needs to be shed by your hands, baby," Saige observed as Kyree allowed Tyrell's limp and bloody body to slump to the floor in a pile of groaning, whimpering limbs. Kyree knelt down next to Saige, brushing the out of place strands of lilac hair back behind her ears, pressing a soft kiss to her forehead.

"Are you OK, my dear?" Kyree's voice was much gentler than usual, com-passionate, a tone he reserved only for Ambrose.

"How did you know?" Saige croaked, her eyes watery as the full extent of her near murder finally hit.

"We didn't," Ambrose answered simply, "we were just stood on the balcony of our room together and Abigor took over. I think he knew, he does seem infatuated with you. Somehow, you must have subconsciously called out to him and he heard."

"I told you Tyrell was-" Kyree began but was silenced abruptly from one well-placed glare from his fiance, "why did he attack you, my dear?" Kyree didn't really care for the reason, was simply content with the justified excuse to mutilate Tyrell beyond recognition.

"He was talking about Idella being poisoned, said he thought that maybe if your parents had been there then you wouldn't have been hurt so bad. I know you never announced that Idella specifically was poisoned, only that one of your family had been taken ill," Saige allowed herself to truly begin crying then, horrified at her own willingness to wallow in self-pity, "I'm sorry, Kyree, you warned me not to be with him, you both did, but I didn't believe you. He was just so sweet and he was the first man to take interest in me and-" Saige succumbed to her sobs, taking great hiccuping breaths as Ambrose rubbed his hand gently across her back. Kyree covered Saige's hand with his own and a feeling of immense calm rolled over her, snuffing out the fear and heartache from within her. She stared incredulously at her father, who had a bemused expression on his face at his daughter's sudden change.

"How are you doing that?" Saige whispered when she finally found her voice again.

"Doing what?" Kyree felt Saige's grip increase when he moved to let go of her hands.

"Making the fear go away, making me calm," at Saige's comment, Ambrose reached out and placed his hand on Kyree's shoulder, a frowning forming on his face.

"I can feel it too, it's a calming effect, has this ever happened before, Ky?" Kyree opened his mouth to answer but didn't get the chance to speak. Instead, he was yanked back as Tyrell, somehow, found the strength to wrap a long, thin piece of metal around his throat. With one well-placed elbow back against Tyrell's shattered rib cage, the twine around Kyree's neck loosened and his attacker crumpled backwards, once again whimpering from the pain.

"Give it up, Tyrell, you're fucking pathetic," Kyree seethed, calling Osiris and Anubis to retrieve the quivering mess that probably could no longer be even considered as a demon.

"I'm gonna bury you next to my brother when he kills you," Tyrell spat as he was dragged from the room, his darkened eyes locked with Kyree's.

"Drop the brother card already," Kyree muttered with a roll of his eyes, "it was five years ago, get over it."

Chapter 30

<hr>

"Must you drag me to this?" Kyree whined, surveying Ambrose's body as he changed into a pair of deep red sweatpants and a black t-shirt that hugged his figure, "I'd much rather we spent today alone, someone didn't let me get much sleep last night."

"Are you complaining about last night?" Ambrose cocked an eyebrow at his fiance, who was smirking back at him silently, "I didn't think so. And you have to come with me because I refuse to pick anyone who isn't as good as you. After what happened to Saige last week, we need better security," Kyree's playful mood was snuffed out as the thoughts of Tyrell Kaine returned to his mind.

"OK, you have a point," Kyree agreed as Ambrose threw a pair of black sweatpants and a matching black t-shirt, instructing him to change quickly or else they would be late.

"You're the king, babe, you're allowed to be late," Kyree purposefully took his time getting changed, not enjoying the prospect of helping Ambrose choose a knight. He had trained for the job for a long time, seeing someone else get it was difficult for him.

"Hey, you OK?" Ambrose cupped Kyree's cheek, noticing his fiance's silent and stony demeanour, "we talked about this, baby," Kyree forced a lopsided smile, resting his own hands on Ambrose's hips.

"I know, I'm fine," Kyree knew Ambrose would see right through his lie but tried it anyway, "we better get going, since you don't want to be late," thankfully, Ambrose didn't continue to pester Kyree, instead simply walked with him through the endless hallways, an arm draped loosely around his fiance's waist.

Ambrose led Kyree to a much larger home gym type room. Osiris and Anubis were stood either side of the doors as they entered, surveying the cluster of men and women hoping to win the position of being Ambrose's knight. They had been talking previously but had fallen silent the second their eyes landed on Ambrose and Kyree.

"Good morning," Ambrose said simply, a flurry of nods being his only reply. Kyree chuckled softly, everyone was so deathly afraid to speak to Ambrose, some were even avoiding eye contact, but they had no qualms for staring at Kyree.

"I was not expecting so many of you, maybe this will last longer than I had assumed," Ambrose's gaze flickered across the demons before him, "each of you have been training to be a knight of hell for the majority of your lives, today only one of you will get that position. So, let us begin," Ambrose instructed each to fight another of the same build and stature, weaselling out the weaker ones easily. That left them with only 7, 2 women and 5 men. Ambrose stood from his place on Kyree's lap, tugging his fiance up as well, who had previously been daydreaming of being somewhere more interesting.

"You have all proved you are better than your equals, but the true test is if you can beat my fiance, Kyree, the only demon worthy of being a knight in my eyes," the remaining demons surveyed Kyree, looking for non-existent weak points to exploit. Kyree hadn't trained recently, but his body had not forgotten what it had been taught. His muscles were strong and well defined, and his reflexes rivalled that of a lion. He doubted many, if any, would beat him.

"Hold my ring, babe," Kyree dropped his beautiful engagement ring into Ambrose's outstretched palm, pressing a chaste kiss to his fiance's lips before taking to the mat against one of the two female demons.

The first three demons were easy pickings for Kyree, getting through them in less than 15 minutes. The fourth and fifth actually put up a better fight, but still succumbed to Kyree's superior techniques. As the sixth took his position opposite Kyree, he had a smug smirk on his lips, Kyree knew it would be quite satisfying to slap that look right off his face.

"I've heard of you," the demon began, "the infamous Kyree Landon. Slaughterer, murderer, faggot," Kyree didn't even have time to get angry before Abigor took his place, fuelled by Ambrose's rage. The demon's offensive demeanour crumbled, he had obviously heard of Abigor too.

The final demon awaiting his turn to fight backed away slightly, never taking his eyes from Abigor as the beast growled softly, his darkened stare on the offending creature in front of him. Other demons that had lost but lingered to observe who became the knight also stepped back, not wanting to get caught in Abigor's line of fire.

The demon didn't stand a chance against Abigor. He scrambled backwards as Abigor's hand reached out and grasped his shoulder, tugging him closer to the creature. Apologies spilt from the demon's mouth as he tried to plead for his life. Abigor didn't care, the demon had offended his Masters, he deserved worse than death.

There was a loud crunching sound of bone-shattering as the demon's skull caved in under Abigor's hand. Blood seemed to spatter on everything, most caught on Abigor's torso and arms as the corpse fell to the mat. Abigor wrung his hands together, collecting the pieces of bone and brain into his palms before shaking it onto the floor with soft splattering sounds that made quite a few of the other demons in the room feel queasy.

"And you say I have a temper," Kyree murmured as he and Ambrose replaced Abigor, "come here," Kyree engulfed Ambrose in a hug, content that Ambrose reciprocated instantly, burying his face in the crook of Kyree's neck as he took long, laboured breaths.

"May I just say, Your Majesties," Kyree glanced up to see the final demon he had yet to fight with a soft smile on his face, "that was pretty fucking awesome," Kyree chuckled softly at the demon's comment.

"Your name?"

"Farell. Farell Birk," Ambrose's head shot up at the demon's comment, his eyes scrutinizing the male stood not too far away from them.

"Your father was Lionel Birk?" the demon nodded, a glint of pride in his eyes, "he was my father's knight, I knew him fondly growing up. I'm so sorry for your loss, he was a noble man," Farell nodded curtly, his gaze faltering slightly, when Ambrose's attention turned to Kyree, "Lionel gave his life to protect my father... well, actually to protect me. I was only young, and there was a group of lesser demons growing restless, not agreeing with the way my father was ruling. They ended up storming the palace and, to spare you the details, Lionel died ensuring no harm came to me. I will be eternally grateful," Kyree smiled warmly, glancing toward Farell, who was clearly biting back a few tears.

"Well, let's see if you live up to your father's legend," Ambrose peppered a few kisses to Kyree's lips, muttering something about love, before moving back off the mat. Farell's build rivalled that of Kyree's, his arms and torso covered in thickened muscles. He had styled chocolate brown hair that matched his not overtly bushy beard and was almost covered in ink. Kyree actually found the man quite attractive, but he came nowhere close to Ambrose's beauty.

Kyree barely dodged the fist thrown at him, roused instantly from his thoughts as two more narrowly missed him. It was quite a few minutes before either actually landed a hit. It was when Farell's left fist came into contact with Kyree's jaw that he felt the brand begin to glow. Wiping away the blood from his lip and holding one hand out to Ambrose, Kyree focused his swimming gaze.

"I'm fine, babe," Kyree murmured, ensuring Ambrose didn't summon Abigor and tear apart Farell as well. Farell moved in to land another hit but as he lifted his fist the doors to the gym swung open.

A petite woman stumbled in, muttering something over and over, her pale blue eyes wild with fear. Her gaze flittered over the demons in the room as if she was searching for something in particular. Osiris and Anubis tensed, but Ambrose waved them away, stepping closer to the frightened woman.

"Are you alright, my dear? How did you get into this building?" Ambrose asked gently, catching the woman's attention.

"A-Are you K-Kyree Landon?" she stammered, her face contorted into an expression of agony, yet also looking as if she was on the precipice of blacking out, "I-I need Kyree L-Landon," her entire body was pale and trembling as a tear trickled down her ashen cheek.

"No, my dear, what do you need Kyree for?" the woman opened her mouth to speak but her legs gave out from under her before she could. Ambrose caught her easily, lowering her to the ground, repeating his question, hoping for a cognitive answer before she passed out.

"He's..." the woman's eyelids were drooping as she tried desperately to remain awake, "he's my father..." she whispered just as her body gave out and she finally succumbed to the dark abyss.

Chapter 31

K yree remained silent as he carried the woman to his and Ambrose's shared bedroom, his fiance following at his heel talking with Farell. Ambrose had confirmed that what the woman had said was true, Kyree was her father, his initials were clear across her chest.

"I didn't turn her," Kyree clarified as he stared down at the slumbering woman, he could feel Ambrose's stare burning into the back of his neck, "I wouldn't, not without talking to you. Not after what happened last time," Kyree leant back into Ambrose when his fiance's hands began kneading the flesh of his shoulders gently.

"I know, baby, I know. But someone did, and with your blood too.""The assassin?"

"Could be. He could have collected your blood from the coronation party, when you broke the wine glass. It only takes a drop to turn a human if they are strong enough," Kyree sighed, his brows knotting into a deep frown.

"Why would someone want to make me another daughter? What do they have to gain from that?"

"I'm not sure, baby. I'm going to take Farell up to the human world and see if we can find anything about the girl," Ambrose held up a small laminated ID card, "her name is Avis, she was born in Los Angeles. We should be able to find something out about her, if only a family to notify of her death," Kyree made a small, frustrated noise, hanging his head in his hands.

"This isn't how you are supposed to turn someone. They are supposed to want it, not have this forced on them. Who would do this? It's sick, it's sadistic," Ambrose knelt in front of his fiance, trailing his fingers up and down Kyree's tense arms.

"Hey, this isn't your fault, Ky," Kyree chuckled bitterly.

"Of course it's my fault, someone is doing this to fuck with me. Some girl just lost her life because someone wants to make me feel worse," Ambrose tilted Kyree's head up with his forefinger and thumb, forcing his fiance to make eye contact with him.

"Stop it. Stop blaming yourself. You didn't turn her. She may have been turned with your blood but she's lucky in that sense. She has a wonderful father now, and she will live in luxury here with us if she so pleases. If not, she may leave any time, either way, you are not at fault. OK?" Kyree contemplated Ambrose's comment for a moment before pressing a chaste kiss to his fiance's lips.

"I love you, be careful," Kyree said, in a much brighter mood.

"I love you too, baby," Ambrose uttered his farewell as he exited the room, leaving Kyree alone to await his new daughter's awakening.

Just over an hour passed before Kyree noticed movement in the girl. Her eyes fluttered open and Kyree immediately noted the crippling fear in her blue iris'. Kyree instantly leant forward, resting his hand over the girl's wrist, feeling the calm aura flow through him and into her.

He wasn't sure what that new found power was, or where it had come from, but it sure as hell came in handy. He had been working on controlling it since it had appeared when consoling Saige and was grasping slowly how to call upon it.

"Hey, you're safe, Avis, you're OK," Kyree ensured his tone was soft, soothing, as he spoke to the girl. She looked young, late teens if he had to guess. Her hair was a beautiful light shade of brown, hanging in straight locks that framed her gaunt face. Her skin was much more tanned than that of Saige's, yet still was a pale shade, matching her sharp and well-defined features.

"H-How do you know my name? A-Are you Kyree?" her voice was trembling and broken, much alike her body in a sense.

"Yes, Avis, I am Kyree. You happened to have an ID card on you that my fiance took, that's how I know your name. Do you know what happened to you?" Kyree attempted to increase the degree of calm he was projecting onto her but was unsure if it even made a difference.

"Not really," her voice sounded a little more even, no longer shaking, maybe Kyree had more control over his power than he thought, "I was dancing with some guy in a club and he took me out the back and then..." she paused, obviously collecting her fragmented thoughts, "then nothing. It's just blurry until I woke up in some hallway knowing I had to find Kyree Landon. Why did I need to find you again? Where are we?" now, that was a difficult question Kyree had never thought he would have to answer. They were demons, in hell. It was not an easy concept for someone to grasp. Yet, as Kyree set out explaining what had likely happened to Avis, she didn't seem all that phased by the idea. Kyree even removed his hand from her wrist, wondering if it was his calming aura that was affecting her. No, she just simply understood.

"So, you're my dad now?" she asked when Kyree had finally finished his long-winded explanation.

"Yes. Although, I didn't intend to take another daughter. I'm deeply sorry you were forced into this world when you didn't ask for this.""Don't be sorry, my life wasn't all that much better before," Avis turned over her arm, revealing a myriad of track marks on her inner elbow both old and new, "heroin addict. I was probably one needle away from OD'ing. I guess whoever turned me saved my life," Kyree grimaced, running his fingers gingerly over the scars, acknowledging each one in turn.

"I hope I can give you a better life then, Avis. I would love for you to remain here with me and my family. We would welcome you, care for you, even love you. You may stay, or, should it truly be your wish, you may leave and live on your own. Either way, I will allow you to decide."

"Tell me about your family," Avis' voice had become soft, a little glimmer of something in her eye that Kyree couldn't quite pinpoint.

"Well, I am engaged to Ambrose Ross, the king of hell. My parents are Yennifer and Orion Landon and my brother is Idella. I also have another daughter, of whom I turned by my own hand at her request, called Saige," Avis seemed to beam at the prospect of joining Kyree's family, but still looked rather sheepish, "you do not have to make your decision immi-nently. Please, take your time to think about it," Kyree rose to his feet, about to speak again when there was a soft knock on the door, "enter," a small, frail-looking woman peeked her head around the door, avoiding eye contact with Kyree.

"Sir," she seemed terrified, her entire body shaking along with her words, "Sir, I'm sorry to burden you with such news but His Majesty has been gravely injured," Kyree felt the blood drain from his face, a cold numbness spreading throughout his body in its place.

"What?" he choked out, his throat closing up and his chest tightening at the prospect of Ambrose being hurt, "What. Happened?" he managed to utter through gritted teeth, his eyes darkening as he glowered at the female staff member.

"I-I don't know, Sir, I-I'm sorry. All I know is Farell is with him in the human world."

"Get out," Kyree seethed, sending the woman scurrying from the room. Dragging his hand through his hair, Kyree remembered Ambrose still had his engagement ring. Emptiness suddenly swelled within him, merely from the ring not adorning his finger.

"What are you waiting around for?" Avis queried, rising to her feet, "go to him, I'm fine here, honestly," Kyree would have smiled at his new daughter's resilience, were it not for the gut-wrenching fear consuming him.

"Oh my God, dad, I just heard about Amb," Saige bustled into the room, flinging her arms around her father and tugging him into a hug, "we have to go see him.""I can't leave Avis alone here, you have to stay with her," Kyree peeled Saige off him tenderly, turning his attention back to Avis, "Avis, this is Saige, your... sister, should you choose to stay."

"Introductions and pleasantries later, dad," Saige said restlessly, "bring her with us, I'll keep an eye on her, I promise," it took pleading from Saige and even a little input from Avis to finally convince Kyree to bring them both. They appeared outside a hospital under the blazing sun in Los Angeles. None had the time to even comment on the beautiful weather as Kyree breezed into the building in search of his fiance. The receptionist said room 375, which Kyree did not understand but Saige and Avis seemed to know where to go.

"Kyree, you have to understand-" Kyree cut off Farell with a single punch, breaking his nose.

"I will deal with you later," Kyree growled, ignoring the smouldering pain in his hand as he entered Ambrose's room. He bit down on his lip as his eyes landed on his fiance, his body broken and bruised. He was covered in gauze and bandages, with wires attached to him as he breathed very slowly.

"Oh, babe," Kyree whispered, perching on the chair nearby the bed, grasping Ambrose's hand and peppering it with tender kisses, "open those eyes for me, Amb, please," he mumbled, tears stinging his eyes as they flittered over Ambrose. Allowing his calm aura to flow into Ambrose, Kyree hoped he would drown out some of the pain his fiance was experiencing. He stayed there, deadly still next to Ambrose, for hours, just simply watching him. Once his anger had finally died down enough, he managed to step out of the room, granting Saige and Avis time alone with their father.

"What happened?" Kyree asked Farell, only just noticing that he too looked in pretty bad shape.

"We were just leaving, decided to walk down an alleyway so humans didn't see us. Bad idea," Farell chuckled bitterly, staring at the floor, avoiding Kyree's eye, "we were jumped by some human men. They were filming us, sick fucks, so we couldn't just disappear. There were so many, and they were screaming at him, screaming awful things. They held me down, didn't do much to me, it was Ambrose they wanted."

"Why?" was the only word Kyree managed, tears in his eyes at the images of Ambrose being hurt haunting his thoughts.

"I don't know, they were just shouting really homophobic stuff. I assumed they knew he was gay, or thought it because we were walking together. Either way, it was awful. Some other humans got them to stop, called an ambulance. I managed to slip him some devil's snare before they noticed, I'm so sorry, Kyree. I failed, I failed on my first fucking day," Farell hung his head in his hands, sighing deeply. Kyree rested his hand on Farell's shoulder, trying to brush away the images of snapping his neck from his mind.

"You didn't fail. You thought quickly, with the devil's snare. Am I mad? Livid is a more accurate word, but he's alive. And he will heal, so you did your job, don't spend your life dwelling on one mistake. Trust me, it doesn't fulfil anything."

Chapter 32

Kyree spent the rest of his evening simply laying with Ambrose. He wanted to be there when his fiance awoke, wanted to ensure he was calm and pain-free. Kyree had sent Farell away with his daughters, instructing them to go have some dinner whilst Ambrose rested.

"Ky?" Kyree looked toward Ambrose, a smile weaving its way onto his mouth.

"Yeah, babe?"

"I want you," Ambrose's raspy voice tore into Kyree's heart, his tone matched his body; beaten and broken.

"You're hurt, we're not fucking right now, you're also on a lot of pain meds, you probably don't even know what you're feeling," Kyree trailed his fingers absently through Ambrose's dark locks, his dark eyes locked onto the drug-dazed ones of his lover.

"Kyree, I may be higher than heaven right now but I know what an erection feels like," Kyree chuckled softly, noticing that Ambrose wasn't embellishing, "I want you," he repeated, his eyes swirling with a mixture of lust and love.

"Ambrose you're in no position to fuck right now, you can barely move."

"Fuck me, Kyree," Ambrose said more forcefully, a little exasperation laced into his quiet tone. Kyree was a little taken aback by Ambrose's desire, he had never been anything other than a bottom before. He wasn't really a dominant personality in the bedroom.

"What?" Ambrose sighed, wincing a little at the effort.

"You fuck me, Kyree. Do you need me to draw you a picture? Put your co-"

"I know, Ambrose, no need for a full explanation," Ambrose smirked weakly as Kyree sat up, his eyes roaming his fiance's injured form, "are you sure? I don't want to hurt you any more than you already are."

"Kyree, I'm aching, OK? Just fuck me," Ambrose's tone resembled a plea, turning Kyree on massively. He could get used to his begging for more. Kyree was careful to remove what little clothes remained on Ambrose's body, allowing his fingertips to graze over his bruised skin as he did so. Ambrose gazed on as Kyree removed his own clothes in a much swifter manner and positioned himself where he needed to be.

"Um, are you...have you ever..." Kyree wasn't sure how to ask the most simple of questions, however, Ambrose found his flustered nature extremely attractive.

"Yes, in this sense, Kyree, I'm a virgin," Kyree leant down and covered Ambrose's mouth with his own, gaining a soft groan of appreciation. Gingerly, Ambrose lifted his aching arms and rested them over Kyree's broad shoulders, one caressing the back of his neck and the other sinking into his thick brunette hair.

A soft whimper slipped from Ambrose as Kyree moved above him ever so slowly, despite how strong the urge was to bury himself to the hilt in his fiance. Kyree focused on his breathing, resting his head in the crook of Ambrose's neck as he awaited his fiance's adjustment to the odd feeling.

"You OK?" Kyree whispered, feeling Ambrose's body tense all over, knowing his back would be littered with scratches for days to come. He enjoyed that thought, a mark from his fiance.

"Yes," Ambrose's voice was so soft, yet so God damn husky Kyree could feel the vibrations of each word resonate through his fiance's neck. Kyree gradually picked up the pace, adoring the soft moans escaping his fiance, similar to the mewls of a newborn kitten.

Neither lasted very long, finishing at the same time, with their lips connected. Kyree, in his sated state, laid back on the bed next to Ambrose, tugging him gently so he snuggled his body into Kyree's. Kyree would never admit it, but either being held or holding Ambrose after making love were his favourite few moments. The intimacy lingered for days, reminding him of the love he shared with his demon.

Days passed achingly slow as Ambrose dwelled in the human hospital. Farell had said it was a better idea than just taking off, at least there whilst Ambrose was healing he could be given medication. When they did finally move him back down to the palace, Farell barely left his side, obviously consumed by the guilt of not doing more to help in his king's time of need.

"You're looking well, Kyree," Kyree glanced up at the familiar voice, not particularly happy with the figure stood before him.

"What are you doing here, Deacon?" Kyree made sure to slick his tone with exasperation, hoping that Deacon would get the hint quickly that he was not wanted.

"I came to see Ambrose, wanted to make sure he's OK after the incident with the humans."

"He's not taking visitors at the moment," Kyree returned his attention to the email he was writing for Ambrose. Any time he wasn't with his fiance, he was trying his best to complete the tasks Ambrose would if he were well.

"Oh, come on, Kyree, I was engaged to the man. Let me see him, just for a few minutes?" Kyree sighed, he wouldn't be able to do anything if Deacon continued pestering him.

"Fine, just let me finish this email," Kyree huffed, trying to ignore the impending headache he felt rolling over him.

"Y'know, Kyree, people do tend to get hurt around you a lot. There's a word for it, oh God, what is it now?" Deacon paused and Kyree revelled in the few seconds of sheer peace and quiet, "a black dog. That's what you are, Kyree, a black dog," Kyree froze in his place, thankful his gaze was on the laptop screen and not Deacon. It had to be a coincidence. It had to be.

"What did you just call me?" Kyree uttered stiffly, trying desperately to keep his voice level.

"Oh, come on, don't get offended by that little comment, Kyree, I've called you so much worse. I was just flirting. A black dog, someone who walks hand in hand with the grim reaper, a sign of impending doom. A death omen," Kyree's hands were trembling, from fear or anger, he couldn't quite depict.

"Deacon, you don't care for Ambrose, why are you really here?" Kyree asked through gritted teeth, focusing on his breathing.

"OK, you got me, Kyree. I'm not really here to see our dear Ambrose. You know me, I do love to feed off your agony," it wasn't a coincidence. How had they not known? Events clicked together like pieces of a puzzle, it all made sense. Deacon Rome was the assassin.

He had to remain calm, maybe Deacon didn't know he knew. No, that was stupid, of course, he knew, he was merely toying with Kyree. Building up his anger, fuelling the fire within him, waiting for the explosion.

"You should really leave, Deacon, I'm not really in the mood for your shit today," Kyree muttered, wracking his brain for some foolproof way to incapacitate the demon who had been terrorizing his fiance and him for months. Ambrose was sleeping just a few doors down, too far away to summon Abigor, too weak to defend himself. Farell was in there with him, but Kyree wasn't sure he could win against Deacon.

There was a dagger in the top drawer to Kyree's left, if he could reach that maybe he would stand a chance. With one quick glance upward, Kyree saw Deacon had moved much closer, his dark eyes intent on Kyree. He had one chance...

Kyree felt the blade on his throat before he even made an attempt to move. Deacon chuckled softly, running his finger down Kyree's cheek, pressing the blade close enough to nick Kyree's skin.

"That truly was amusing to watch, Kyree, dear," Deacon's voice dripped with a smug tone, further irritating Kyree, "your thoughts are a wonderful source of entertainment."

"My thoughts?" Kyree felt the blade press closer to his skin as he spoke, keeping his comment short and succinct.

"I can read minds, Kyree, my dear, how do you think I am so powerful? I knew Ambrose would be staying at your mansion, I knew when you were in the human world, I knew when either of you were alone. It truly is the most coveted gift," Deacon taunted.

"So, what now? You got me right where you want me, kill me. What's the point toying with me?"

"I told you, I enjoy your agony. And, you're my little bargaining chip."

"You need a bargaining chip for?"

"To get to Ambrose of course," Kyree felt a twinge of panic jolt through his chest but tried his best to keep his mind blank, "shall we?" Deacon forced Kyree to his feet, walking him out of the office.

"Why are you doing this? What are you going to achieve by murdering the king of hell, Deacon? You'll be caught, no one will let you get away with it," Deacon's chuckle was low and sinister.

"Well, before you ruined my God damn engagement, I would have been king," Deacon's tone grew darker as he allowed rage to take over for a few seconds, "but now, when Ambrose dies, I'll get the simple satisfaction that I killed him."

"What makes you think I'll let you kill him?" Kyree seethed, feeling his horns grow, regretting it when Deacon wrapped his hand around one, tightening his grip until Kyree let a soft whine slip from his pursed lips.

"Because, Kyree, I will give you two options, of which I already know the one you will choose," Deacon stopped outside of Ambrose's bedroom, instructing Kyree to open the door, "either, I kill him now, quick and painless, sparing him the agony of watching you be killed too. Or I kill you in front of him, then leave him to suffer alone until he inevitably kills himself after months of unhealthy grieving," Kyree growled softly as he opened the door, walking in first, instantly alerting Farell.

"Let go of him," Farell hissed, his eyes seeping to a soulless black as he moved to block Ambrose from Deacon's view.

"Tick tock, Kyree, pick an option," Ambrose looked peaceful as he slept, a small frown on his face. He wasn't dreaming, Kyree could sense that, but the simple blankness he was experiencing was tranquil and soothing. He couldn't put Ambrose through the grief he had experienced himself, not after everything else he had put his poor fiance through.

"Him first," Kyree whispered, a tear trickling down his cheek, defeat filling him. Something cold and sharp was pressed into his left hand and sorrow swelled within him.

"No, I'm not doing it," Kyree let the dagger slip from his fingers and clatter to the floor, "I'm not giving you that kind of satisfaction, not now, not ever."

"Well, looks like you're dying first then," Deacon turned his attention to Farell, "wake him, now.""I don't take orders from you," Farell shot back. Kyree didn't need the ability to read minds to know that Farell was flicking through every scenario in his mind, searching for the one that would involve the least amount of death.

"Do it, Farell," Kyree whispered, an awful feeling of defeat growing within him. As Farell set about waking Ambrose, a deep frown on his face, Kyree felt Deacon tense behind him.

"Drop the knife," Kyree heard a female voice utter, then Deacon chuckled, allowing the dagger to slacken in his grip enough for Kyree to step away. Kyree spun on his heel, a shot of pride expelling all desperation from him.

"Avis," Deacon still had a smug expression on his face, even in death he still believed he was the most intelligent in the room, "my dear child, you really don't know what you are getting yourself into. Maybe settling you in here was not my best idea, of course you would grow to love Kyree as Kyree loves you, it was a rash move that I should have really thought more about."

"You used Kyree's blood to turn me?" Avis held a blade to Deacon's throat, Kyree could see the strain as she leant up, trying to remain the same height as the assassin.

"Oh, that is hilarious, my dear. I didn't use Kyree's blood. I used my own. You are my daughter, Avis, not Kyree's," Avis' stance faltered for just second as what Deacon had said set in.

"You can't be serious, it's my mark on her chest, Deacon. You're not her sire."

"The size of the mark doesn't matter, we demons just like to flaunt what we own. Look under the L, you will see my initials. Go ahead, take a look," removing the dagger from Deacon's outstretched hand, Kyree examined the bottom of the L over Avis' heart, despair infecting his mind at the sight of it.

"He's telling the truth Avis," Kyree muttered softly, "you can't kill him, you'll die too," Kyree stepped back, glancing over at Ambrose to see him awake and cognisant but silent as ever.

"But the threat to you and Ambrose will be gone if I kill him?" Kyree's gaze snapped back to Avis, her pale blue eyes holding tears on the rims.

"Avis, it isn't worth it. We have ways to make the rest of his eternity worse than death. There is no need for you to give your life for us."

"But keeping him locked up, there will always be a chance of him escaping, a chance of him recruiting others to his cause through rumours or corrupt demons. If I kill him, you're safe. You're both safe," Kyree noted desperation in her eyes, fear swirling with sorrow in the beautiful blue hue of her iris'.

"Avis, it isn't worth it. Please, this is what he wants, this is his final ploy. Avis, you mean more to us than safety. Drop the knife," Kyree held out his hand for the knife but Avis merely pressed it closer to Deacon's throat, nicking the skin slightly.

"In the few days I was with you, Kyree, you made me truly feel a part of something. In my human life, never had I ever felt so loved. I can't think of a better way to repay you," Avis ignored Kyree's pleas for her to stop, her vision becoming blurred with tears as she uttered one last whisper, "I love you, dads."

Epilogue

Kyree felt as though his heart would burst from his chest it was beating so fast. The incessant thumping of his blood pounding in his ears seemed to be slowly driving him insane as he tried to control his breathing. He felt nauseous, light headed and unsteady all at the same time, wondering whether he would truly pass out as he had been repeating all morning.

"Dad, you look a little pale, are you OK?" Saige queried, running the back of her hand down Kyree's cheek, catching his attention, "breathe, dad, it's all gonna go fine," Saige sounded as reassuring as possible, but it made no difference to Kyree. He was still shaking, still weak at the knees, still paralyzed by fear.

"I don't know if I can do this," Kyree admitted, inhaling deeply as he had been instructed to when he felt his terror rising to an insurmountable point. He stared at his reflection in the mirror, noting how sickly pale he looked, his bewitching hazel and grey-blue eyes swirling with anxiety.

"Dad, when we first met you practically ripped apart the men trying to hurt me. You have been through loss, grief and depression. Your wedding day should not scare you this much, this isn't going to turn out like your last,

OK?" Kyree attempted some form of smile, hoping Saige understood what she was saying had an effect, even if it was minute. A soft knock at the door caught the two demon's attention as it swung open slightly.

"Dad, they're saying it's time," Avis smiled compassionately at her father as the three walked together from the room. Avis and Saige were both wearing matching elegant burgundy gowns that flowed down their bodies and just brushed against the carpet ever so slightly.

The two daughters stopped with Kyree at the corner just before the aisle, awaiting the music to begin. In that time, Kyree had allowed his calming aura to slip out, relaxing the two of them as they slipped their arms into his. Kyree had opted to be given away by his two children, rather than his parents. Nothing about the wedding was truly traditional, Kyree had specified no similarities to his previous wedding.

"You look really handsome, dad," Avis whispered, leaning up to kiss her father's cheek. In the months that had followed from Deacon being captured, Avis had grown much closer with her fathers, despite being blood to neither of them. In turn, it had not been Kyree's pleas for Avis to leave Deacon alive but rather Ambrose's that had struck her hard enough to have mercy on the assassin and value her life higher than that of Kyree and Ambrose's imminent safety.

"Yeah, Amb is gonna be blown away," Saige mirrored her sister, returning to her original position just as the music began. Ambrose had chosen Love by Lana Del Ray for Kyree to walk down the aisle to, having somehow remembered that that was the song that had played when he turned the stereo on in Kyree's apartment the first night they met.

Oddly, Kyree made no hesitation, instantly setting off at a slow pace down the aisle, trying to keep his focus solely on his soon to be husband. He could sense eyes on him, every demon in the grand hall staring directly at Kyree, their gazes burning into him.

But Kyree merely kept his attention trained on Ambrose stood waiting at the end of the aisle for him. His fiance was adorning a wondrous smile, filled with warmth and compassion and love. One that made all fear dissipate within Kyree as he neared Ambrose.

"You look gorgeous," Ambrose whispered as Kyree's hands were placed gently onto his by their daughters.

"Shut it," Kyree murmured, a soft smile taking place on his own lips, "you'll make me cry."

Kyree barely remembered what he had said for his vows, too busy gazing lovingly at Ambrose for the duration of the ceremony. Now, as the two strolled out onto the balcony, hand in hand, wanting to steal a moment of peace together from the crowd inside, he couldn't help tugging his husband close.

"I love you, Ambrose Ross," Kyree muttered, glancing down at the rings on their fingers. Their wedding bands were utterly breathtaking. A gold band outlined a matte black strip down the middle with golden tree branching standing out against the obsidian background.

"I love you too, Kyree Ross," Ambrose replied, capturing Kyree's mouth in a passionate kiss as their fingers locked together, their skin brushing against the cold metal rings.

"I'm sorry to interrupt," Lucifer stood in the doorway to the balcony, looking a little sheepish, "I just wanted to give you your wedding gift in person, out here away from everyone," Lucifer stepped closer to the two newlyweds, holding out a dog-eared and faded envelope with their names written upon the yellowing paper.

"Father, you didn't have to," Ambrose took the envelope, a smile on his lips, opening it with care.

"My gift to you is my knowledge. I know you will have many questions, and I will be happy to answer them for you. I also know you may be angry with me for not confiding all this in you before but you have to understand that I couldn't interfere with this," Ambrose and Kyree shared a bemused look, before unfurling the letter and reading the short prose written upon it.

To Ambrose Bronwen and Kyree Draven,

Our beautiful boys, if you are reading this letter then you must have matured into wonderful young men and no doubt the bond between the two of you has been consummated. You will have questions, we understand that, and we will be happy to answer each and every one in detail when we meet again. But, for now, we shall keep this letter short. You are different, you must have noticed that by this time. The bond that links the two of you is like no other and will forever remain at the strength in which you feel at this very moment. The lives you have lived, we are afraid to inform you, are that of lies, pure fabrication created to ensure the safety of you both and your brothers until you were able to defend yourselves. We did not wish this life of separation upon you, this was not the way we intended for you to grow up. What you are is a much more complicated matter that cannot be explained in the few words we are able to scrawl down for you. What we cannot stress to you enough is that you must remember one word and one word only if all else fails you. You are not demons, Kyree and Ambrose, you are inarmorates. A race so ancient and so hidden that not even millennia old texts write of our existence. Be patient, for we will reunite together with your brothers when all bonds have been connected. For now, we leave you with the knowledge that you are loved, you are cherished and you are meant for something so much bigger than the realm you live in. Be safe, sweet boys.

Love, Yuki Onna Bronwen and Jezebeth Draven.

The words on the pages seemed to jumble in the two men's minds as they tried to understand what they had just read. Glancing at one another then Lucifer, Kyree remained silent but Ambrose somehow found the words to speak.

"Father, what are we?"

Fin.